WAR SONG

LEGACY RISING

MICHAEL MICHEL

MORNINGSTAR BOOKS

CONTENTS

CHAPTER ONE

HERE I GO

- AUTUMN, YEAR 522 A.R. -

Admar spat on the soot-grimed window of the taproom. Yellowed foam raced down the pane of glass. He lifted a bandaged fist and rubbed it clean for better visibility.

"What you doing, Addy?"

Admar ignored Lakka's question. Chair creaking, he leaned closer to the glass and peered out. Scothean soldiers made their way up the street.

"Daydreaming of dead snakes, Lakka." Barnhold's voice was a smooth drawl, the kind of tone where everyone heard him smiling without having to see it. "Does he ever do anything else?"

Admar shrugged. It wasn't far from the truth. Better days with his former lover, Vanique, came to mind on occasion, as did passing moments of laughter with his sister, Ayra. Not now though. Not with *them* so close.

Nine Scoths hustled up the muddy street of Brighthaven, the hafts of their crescent axes gripped tightly in their fists. White cloaks trailed, spattered brown at the hems by filth. But the polished sigil on their chest armor stabbed at Admar's eyes in the fading evening light: a horned serpent coiled around a sun. The symbol of their homeland.

The mark of conquerors.

Admar turned to his friends, fingertips tickling the hilt of a dagger in his belt. Heat pooled in his chest. He'd already let one filthy fucking Scoth taste steel; it was the least he could do to honor Ayra, long dead from an infection earned in the whipping line. Vanique's death, too, was Scothea's fault. She'd contracted slum-sickness a year ago but couldn't afford the herbs she'd needed to fight it. No one could.

Admar tensed. Vanique had deserved a fighting chance at life. *We all do but we've gotta be willing to bloody our hands.*

He had been drunk when he survived his run-in with a lone soldier in a shadowed alley. *A lucky fool, that's all I am. I should count myself happy to be alive and stop there.* But ever since that night when he'd sprinted home and washed the blood off, he'd been eager to share his blade with more of them. His dead sister and former lover would want that.

"Best not to talk about such things out loud, Barnhold." Lakka's chin hovered over her gutter-wine, a drink that cost her a third of her day's earnings. She shot a cautious look at the barkeep but he was preoccupied with cleaning his graying teeth with his tunic sleeve. Scothea controlled everything. Wages, resources...informants. Neighbors had become just as dangerous as a shock trooper's ax since the filthy fucks had conquered the Fractured Lands. "If Scoths hear you talkin' about killin' snakes, they'll send you to the quarries. At best, they'll do that."

"No Scoth would ever be caught dead in a place like this. Drinking flavored piss in the company of miners like us." Barnhold laughed with abrasive dismissal. "Consider yourself safe."

"Safe." Admar eased back into his chair, sparing one final glance at the Scoths who'd slowed to a walk outside. "The mere fact that we're having this conversation should tell you you've lost your damn mind."

The bigger man's brow darkened. Sinewed arms tensed around the cup in his callused palms. A vein on his bald pate pulsed, every fiber of him angry but never letting on to it. His thick mustache twitched over a smile.

A damn fake smile. None of them had anything to be happy about.

"Shirking about in the dark where the Scoths won't see us and clanging pick to stone in a damned cave all the gods' damned day." Admar made a fist and slammed it onto the table, making his drink jump. "Sweating our life out so they can have the sweet and the warm and the prime cut meat of the world. Meanwhile, we drink puddle water and give them everything on a gold platter."

Admar slapped his drink off the table. The tankard thudded to the ground and sloshed onto Barnhold's arm.

The bigger man huffed, wiped the liquid off, then reached across the table to tap the ring left by Admar's gutter-wine. "Nature isn't such a mystery as you make it out to be. No matter how loud a dog barks, an ice tiger will kill it in a scrap every time." He slugged back his drink. Golden beads clung to his wire-covered upper lip. "What good is it doing you to think otherwise?"

Good? I had the balls to kill one of them. No better good than that! He wanted to tell them. He wanted to shout it from the top of Brighthaven's watch towers. He wanted everyone to know.

The Scoths were not gods. They died like normal men.

"Take a cue from me, Addy." Lakka puffed up with pride. "I'm a happy enough woman, no matter the conditions. Family is what's most important. If you've got your health and your loved ones, why stress the other stuff?"

And if your loved ones are dead? What then?

Barnhold shot Lakka a disapproving look.

She blushed but Admar waved a hand. "It's fine. Ancient history by now." It wasn't. The future was a path paved in broken glass; just when he'd become numb to the latest wound, time cut away another piece of him.

Barnhold cleared his throat. "I know you hate 'em for what they did to Ayra—"

"And Vanique." When Scotheans were in charge, suffering tended to come in batches. "That was the worse of the two. A few herbs...." He trailed off.

"Sorry, Addy," Lakka said. "I know you miss them. At least you've still got us. Wish you could see that. Friends is more than most have."

Barnhold gestured at Admar's bandaged hands with his tankard. "Can't see what's in front of you with your eyes up the sky's ass all day, dreaming and fantasizing. That's why you cut yourself on slate so damn much."

"No." A growl crackled at the back of Admar's throat. "I cut myself because Scoths forced my parents to be miners, the same shit I inherited. No choice but to work or die, right?" He searched the faces of his friends. "It sounds like some of us are starting to believe that bullshit. Just remember, when the quota's not hit, you're standing there naked and shivering in the line at my side, waiting for the lash."

Menace poured over Barnhold's words. "We don't. Talk about. The line."

Lakka's face fell to the table. She sniffled.

"I know." Admar felt himself soften some. No one talked about the line. It was a shameful abuse better condemned to its moment and not given another second of life's precious time. "I know we don't. No one talks about the pain." He swallowed hard. "We just accept it. 'Let it go at the grave.' Isn't that what the Kanians say?"

Barnhold gathered himself for a retort, but Lakka stiffened suddenly, silencing them both.

Admar followed her gaze to the window. "Shit."

The nine Scoths were approaching the taproom door. A hooded figure waddled at their center, potbelly pressing the sides of the cloth tight.

"Nobody panic." Barnhold's tongue darted over his lips, smile vanished. "Sit down. Here—get your damn drink. Eyes down, damnit!"

Another patron sprinted from a dark corner to the bar and ducked behind it. Admar snatched his cup from the floorboards and sat, greasy, ruddy hair falling around his face. The barkeep brushed crumbs from his clothes and set to cleaning a tankard. From what Admar could tell, it was likely the first time.

The door opened, hinges shrieking. Cold prickles raced up the back of Admar's skull and arms. His mouth went dry. From the corner of his eye, he watched them file in, all axes and armor and grim expressions. The clatter of their plated skirts brought a pleasant melody to the uninitiated. For those well acquainted with Scothean mercy, the sound meant predators stalked nearer.

The hooded figure came in last. A pair of low-hanging bulges atop her belly marked her as a woman. She turned toward Admar's table.

His eyes flicked down and stayed there, heart galloping.

Booted feet approached, heel-toe, at a leisurely pace. She hung behind Barnhold a moment and then slid over to Lakka, a gnarled, liver-spotted hand claiming her shoulder.

"Little mice." A sibilant whisper struck the wind from Admar's lungs and he had to fight an animal desire to flee the taproom. The woman in the hood crouched low, bringing her face parallel with Lakka's. Stringy gray hair hung around a moon-round face. Bulging gold eyes probed Admar. He looked away.

"Dirty things. And so far from their tunnels." The woman pushed back her hood. Scabbed and festering mounds clung to bald patches like barnacles above one of her ears and down the part in her hair. She took Lakka's drink and sniffed it, then chuckled. "A putrid existence. Should we put them out of their misery, captain?"

"What do you want?" Admar tensed at Barnhold's question.

The woman stared at the brawny miner. "You think yourself strong, don't you?"

Barnhold shook his head. "Merely a question…Mistress."

"Oh? Is it *merely* a question?" She flicked his ear. "And I suppose you want *merely* an answer?"

"Carbuncle," said the Scoth captain. "We've yet to question them."

She ignored the man. "You think because I'm an old woman that I fear a set of big arms, is that it?" Her flabby neck wobbled. Anger stained her cheeks wine-purple. "I've survived horrors you could not imagine. Doled out plenty of the same too. I can show you if you like." Her mouth split into a crooked-toothed grin. "I promise, you won't like it."

The Scoth captain grunted. "We have a mission, Mistress."

"I'm sorry, Mistress," Barnhold said quickly. The strongest among them had been unmanned in less than a minute.

"Fine." The woman, Carbuncle, waved a hand. "Let's do the deed then. I'm eager to be home."

The captain pushed forward and loomed over Lakka. He was tall for a Scoth, his skin tan, his eyes narrow. Lakka sensed him staring down at her, and glanced upward.

"Asenya the Rat." The captain withdrew a roll of soiled parchment, unraveled it, and showed her. "Are you she?" The woman in the drawing shared Lakka's same drab hair and narrow face, but her nose was verminous, her teeth askew where Lakka's own were straight. The similarities could place them as cousins at best. Certainly not the same person. Lips parted, Lakka frowned at the image.

The captain delivered a perfunctory backhand slap across her jaw, evoking a yelp. "Respond or die!"

Tears welled in Lakka's eyes as redness seeped into her cheek.

"No." Barnhold spoke through gritted teeth. "Her name is Lakka."

The captain raised an eyebrow, then looked at Admar. He gulped. "You've got the wrong woman. That's Lakka."

"Very well. The hard way." The captain nodded, a grim and final thing. "Carbuncle."

The hag grinned. Black smoke started rolling from between the gaps in her teeth. "Delightful." A ghostly, dark light seeped from the hideous woman's mouth.

She's not an Awakened. She's one of the mad ones...a Ruptured.

Shadows spread out from the woman, obscuring the light from the windows and casting darkness over Lakka's face. "Last chance to tell the truth." Carbuncle chuckled as if she told a joke. "Are you Asenya the Rat?"

Hands locking together, Lakka stumbled from her chair and onto her knees. Sweat lathered her face and damped her hair. She blubbered for mercy as tears sped down her cheeks. Over and over, she begged and pleaded with them and said her true name. She knew how things like this went. They all knew the way of Scoths.

Carbuncle smiled. "Petty mice. Such liars. We should purge them all." She turned to the captain and shook her head.

The tall Scoth squared his shoulders toward Lakka. "Asenya the Rat, you are hereby charged with the crime of unlawful bartering. With the voice of Count Gulkov of Alistar, and the will of the Sempyrean Gods, your sentence is death."

"Damnit!" Barnhold hissed and tried to stand, but a pair of guards clapped gloved hands onto his shoulders and pinned him in his chair. "You've got the wrong woman!"

A third Scoth placed his ax blade on the back of Admar's neck. "Be smart. Justice only calls for the one."

Justice! Inwardly, a whirlwind of bloody vengeance rose in Admar. Outwardly, he grew a shade paler. Guilt deepened, an everlasting latrine into which his courage was thrown and his cowardice stagnated.

Carbuncle opened her mouth.

A dense black cloud wormed outward, stirring gray strands of hair at the corners of the Ruptured woman's mouth. Quiet and predatory, like a shark stalking a seal through a shoal, it glided from Carbuncle's lips and entered Lakka's cheek.

The miner and mother gasped as if splashed with cold water, then touched her face. She panted, seeming to wonder what had happened. Seeming to hope that nothing bad would come.

But she knew that was not the way of Scoths, nor the way of their Ruptured. Tens of thousands of graves marked the efficiency of their occupation, the mercy of their justice. All of Kania had been forfeited to their thirst for dominance, a once beautiful island now fallen to ash, ruin, and piracy.

Those Kanians who managed to survive were naught but slaves now. And just like Admar, they could do nothing but whine about the injustice of it all.

The flesh under one of Lakka's eyes bubbled. She convulsed, the muscles of her face seeming to come alive with dreadful understanding. Across the table, Barnhold went deathly still, his gaze locking onto their friend as the skin under her eye burst. Flecks of rust-colored ooze exploded from the wound, spackling Carbuncle's face. Lakka screamed and launched herself backward, a futile attempt to escape the burgeoning horror.

Carbuncle licked her lips and cackled. "Not feeling well, sweetie?"

Lakka thrashed on the ground, grabbing at domes of swelling red skin. Crusty boils wept and then popped, accompanied by a sickening sizzle like fat dripping onto a fire. Though it couldn't have taken more than a minute, the moment carved itself eternally into Admar's memory. Eruptions of cantankerous pale skin continued until the vessel of Lakka's sad, brief life lay completely open, a carcass already picked apart by scavengers.

She lay still, runnels of blood pooling around her mangled corpse. Glazed-over eyes stared at the rafters and her mouth held a puddle of crimson. A couple of organs peeked through gaping wounds—these, too, had burst like overripe pumpkins.

A single rattled breath. That was the last thing Admar heard from his friend before she died. A putrid smell filled the back of his throat. His vision dimmed.

"It is done," said the captain. "Shall we return you to the keep, Mistress?"

Carbuncle pivoted, a gnarled hand patting her potbelly. "Indeed, Captain. I'm quite famished."

"That was Lakka..." Admar gaped. "She had children...a husband."

Carbuncle waddled over to Barnhold. Veins writhed along corded, burly forearms.

"That was Lakka," Admar repeated in disbelief. "You killed her."

"A criminal," said the captain. "Asenya the Rat."

Justice was as dim a concept to the Scoths as freedom was to those under their rule. Admar wanted to shake his head but couldn't. The ax touching the nape of his neck sucked the heat from him, its cold blade sending prickles across his scalp. He swallowed hard. *Act like they want you to and you'll make it through this.* The words plunged him lower, to a safe place where he might suffocate in silence. Out of the light. Under their attention. Like a mouse.

Carbuncle bent over her girthy belly so that her mouth was even with Barnhold's ear. "Pissed off about your friend, eh? I've got a warm bed if you want to get some of that aggression out." She brushed his earlobe with flaky, peeling lips. "You wouldn't be the first stallion I break."

A smile stretched beneath Barnhold's mustache, all the tension melting away.

Shit. Admar held his breath.

Barnhold surged to his feet and swiveled around, tankard crashing into Carbuncle's face. Blood burst from her nose as she wilted to the ground. The ax at the back of Admar's neck dragged away in haste, leaving a burning cut. He remained motionless as shouts and chaos unfolded.

Barnhold bulled the two men who'd been pinning him down against the wall, all three going down in a tangle of limbs. Half of the Scoths—including the captain—raced to Carbuncle's aid, while the others hurried to subdue Barnhold with the butts of their axes.

The miner rolled over, booted the nearest Scoth in the knee and sent it bowing back with a crunch. "Come on, Addy!"

Barnhold's summons slashed through Admar but he stayed put, going so far as to stretch himself out farther on the table to appear more submissive.

Barnhold cursed and threw an elbow back into the throat of one of the men on the ground while the other grabbed at him. A soldier slammed the butt of his ax down on Barnhold's torso while the brawler managed to gouge out the eyes of the Scoth holding him back. The man's hands flew to his damaged eyes and the miner wrested the Scoth's ax into his own hands.

He came up swinging as both men on the ground behind him moaned around their injuries. Barnhold's first cut opened a wound on a soldier's thigh. Crimson sluiced onto the floorboards.

At the sight of blood spilled by one of their own, the others reversed their axes in their grips, ax blades over their shoulders. Ready to kill.

It didn't take long. This wasn't a dark alley. Barnhold didn't have a knife or the luck of surprise like Admar had had.

Barnhold plowed forward with wild abandon, heading for Carbuncle where she sat on the ground with a gushing, broken nose between her shaking hands. "Her name was Lakka, you fucks!" The miner came in high—the captain answered a split second faster. He slapped Barnhold's attack aside then buried his ax into the man's guts.

Rather than die whimpering, Admar's friend hunched over the wound, holding his insides in with low, gentle grunts. "Well…" His legs started to shake. Bright red rimmed his teeth and spilled down the crotch of his pants as he grimaced. Somehow, his voice maintained its edge of confidence, though hoarser. "Here I go."

The captain watched him a moment, then nodded to one of his men. Steel flashed, relieving Barnhold of his head. It rolled to a stop, rocking side to side on the back of the skull, his smile and mustache facing Admar, and then jarring away, as if Barnhold shook his head in a final act of disapproval.

Admar lowered his face and stretched his palms farther still until he was prostrate over the table, nose pressed against the mildewed surface. A hollow pit opened in his chest, a mix of grief and jealousy, of friends lost and courage forfeited.

"This one is broken." It was the captain's voice. "He's harmless. Leave him."

While they gathered up their injured and left the taproom, Admar was motion-less. The tears came sometime long after his friends' corpses had gone cold.

Chapter Two

A Feast of Crumbs

T he door shook under Admar's fist. "Joahl."

Within, something scuttled across the floor as if kicked by unsuspecting feet. A quiet curse followed.

"It's important, Joahl." Admar shoved his forehead against the wood. "Please."

A child's voice, asking for water. They received nothing but a harsh whisper.

Admar stepped back and punched a warped slat. The door shuddered, rusted hinges creaking. "For fuck's sake, man! They killed your wife!" Admar surveyed the poor quarter. Even in the dark, with a pall of fog clouding the street, he knew the pair of silhouettes at the end of the lane were Scoth patrolmen.

No one stands so confidently. So unafraid.

The mice, as the Scoths referred to anyone who didn't share their blood, scuttled about with their heads hung low and buried between their shoulders. Admar worked his tongue along his gums, dislodging a sour taste. *I'll show you harmless, you fucking snakes.*

"Joahl," he said, mouth flush with a gap in the frame. "I'll wake everyone in this damn slum if I must. Or you can open the door."

Three angry footsteps later and Lakka's husband jerked it open. He was tall enough that it seemed he held up the ceiling with his cotton cap. Yet, everything else about the man was low, slouched, defeated.

"What do you want?" Joahl shivered. "Be quick. It's cold."

"You know..." Admar drew himself up, then promptly placed a hand against the doorframe to keep his balance for he was good and drunk. He'd blown his entire week's earnings on as many drinks as he needed to drown the words of the Scoth captain after they'd killed Lakka and Barnhold.

This one is broken.

"Aren't you gonna do something?" Admar asked. "They killed your wife."

Joahl's long face leaned out from the house, gaunt eyes slowly searching the streets. The Scoth guards seemed to be standing still—watching them. Joahl noticed. He retracted back into his dingy hovel, a turtle retreating to its shell. "What's there to do?"

"Something," Admar hissed. "Everything. They killed your wi—"

"Not my children," Joahl whispered, his voice obscenely soft. They seemed like the last breathless words of a dying man. Yet this one still stood, heart beating with fear. "Not my children. They left them alive and I'll do anything I must to keep them that way."

"Alive," Admar scoffed. He glanced at his poorly bandaged hands. Spots of amber, where his blood had seeped through and dried, stared back at him. "You call this alive. Give them five years and they'll be working the mines and taking lashes in the town square like the rest of us."

Joahl's tone fell lower, words crawling on their cowardly belly into Admar's ears. "Still alive though, Addy. Still alive." He stepped back, his arm slipping behind the door to shut it. "Forget Lakka. You'll live longer."

How can I? She was innocent! Admar felt like a dog, unable to give up the bone in his jaws. He surged forward, foot blocking the door, his face so close to Joahl's that their noses nearly touched. He meant to say something impactful, something to convince the man to join him in a bid for vengeance, not just for Lakka nor Vanique or Ayra, but for all of those suffering across the Fractured Lands.

Rebellion. Freedom.

But in the end, he just growled like a fool and stepped back into the foggy night. He waved a hand of dismissal at Joahl. The man could be a fighter if he wanted to—they all could—but the only one willing to do anything relevant had taken an ax to the gut three days earlier.

"You're right," Admar mumbled and stumbled into the streets of Brighthaven. "Mice must stay in their nests where it's safe."

A feast of crumbs, that's what he hopes for, and his fear condemns his children to the same. Admar looked over his shoulder. The Scoth patrol split apart and moved off. *Unless I do something about it.*

Admar's heartbeat was in his ears. It was so loud that he feared for a passing, illogical moment that it might alert a guard to his presence. In the dark he waited, dagger gripped at his side. A rough and jagged cornerstone poked his back and hip, snaring the fabric of his cloak.

Muffled steps plodded over the fog-damp grass of the courtyard. Close.

I'll show you harmless.

Brighthaven slept but Admar's wrath had only just awoken. He raised the dagger, elbow cocked. He tried to remember how he'd done it the first time but the memory was a blur in the face of impending violence.

For more than a week, he'd knocked on the doors of friends and acquaintances who'd been wronged by Scothea, only to come to the saddest conclusion of his life: there were no more heroes in the Fractured Lands.

For every door slammed in his face, every sudden shove landing him on his backside, he'd drawn nearer to the truth. He was the only one left. The only one willing to fight.

And he'd need to do so alone.

The gates had been kept open until nightfall, barely guarded. There had been little need to sneak in. What did the Scoths have to fear? The populace was quelled. They *believed* they were mice, inferior in every way. That fact simply deepened his hatred and validated his harrowing choice. He would kill their leaders or die trying. If he could show his brothers and sisters that the Scoths were vulnerable, there might still be a chance.

Polished boots came to the corner of the keep where Admar hid, and stopped. He held little doubt one of his fellow mice shone them daily. He could almost see the poor soul hunched over, eyes darting up at their perceived better to ensure they weren't stoking displeasure.

A muscle in Admar's jaw twitched. *You'll not look down on us again, not after tonight. Come now, just a little farther...*

The toes pivoted away and moved off. He peeked out, spotting the soldier at the center of the grassy courtyard on his way to the twenty-foot palisades beyond. Sharpened tips poked up through a thick band of fog, and after a few heartbeats, the Scoth disappeared into the roiling density of gray.

Relief washed over Admar in a cold wave. The sweat pooling around the collar of his tunic chilled him. Despite his tough talk, he knew the farther he got without conflict, the better his chances of success would be.

He sucked in a slow breath, checked around the corner, then hurried out, staying tight to the shadowed wall of the keep as he made for a dark portal. When he was near enough, the fear of being spotted had him barreling inside in a frantic rush.

A lip of stone snagged his toe. He lurched forward, banging his knee on the third step of the spiraling staircase of a drum tower. A low hiss escaped between his teeth as he clutched his knee. His eyes watered as he tested the leg and found it still worked, though numbly. With all of his weight going into his right leg—the other bearing but a split second of the transition—ascending the stairwell became an arduous task.

Upward he hobbled, dagger at the ready while his other hand traced the fat pillar of the spiraling stairwell. He passed the first floor. Then the second. By the third, his leg was coming back awake, his gait smoothing out.

"She in there?"

Just before the hall of the fourth floor, Admar froze, knife jumping out straight, level with a sliver of entryway a half dozen steps farther on where shadows shifted amidst the flickering torchlight.

A second man answered, more gruff than the first. "The kid from the market too. Hag can't let a pretty face go by without licking her nasty old chops."

Admar's heart thudded against his breastbone. Nature begged him to pant, to force air into his lungs, but he pushed the urge down. A dull ache radiated from the center of his chest. If he gasped now and gave himself away, it might be the last breath he ever drew.

The voices of the men seemed to be holding position. It would be next to impossible to get past them. He needed them to move. Silence pulsed. Pressure built behind his eyes.

"What?" The gruff voice said. "Why are you shaking your head at me?"

"It is not our place to judge her."

"She can't hear us."

The gruff voice harrumphed. "You don't know that. You don't know what she can do. Besides, she outranks you. Keep your mouth shut."

The reprimanded sentry mumbled and cursed, the sound of his voice fading as he moved down the hall.

"Idiot," said the gruff one, now alone.

At least, that's what Admar hoped. *My life depends on it.*

He gave it another minute before he slid up the stairs, careful not to let himself drag along the wall. The hall was dimly lit. When a single silhouette came into view, Admar stopped to gather himself. A dozen paces separated him from the sentry. A heroic dash to liberation.

The captain's face loomed in memory, casual and indifferent. *This one is broken.* He seemed to be addressing a dog rather than a man. But Admar was no dog.

I will teach you what I am.

He drew on the truth of his humanity, the battered and broken feelings left to rot in their cage. Rage lifted him from the muddied depths of abuse. He adjusted the grip on his dagger, then strode up and through the entryway acting as though he were just another sentry.

Disorienting shadow splashed the hall, making it all seem like some nightmarish projection. He felt the soldier's head swivel toward him more than he saw it happen.

"Kerev, is that..." the Scoth's hand fell to his weapon.

Admar soaked up the distance in a rush, knife slashing in wild arcs at the man's neck before he could bring his ax to bear. Flesh parted under his passing blade—once, twice—and then he was stabbing into the bulk of the guard who grunted and gasped as his back stuttered down the wall into a pile.

Hot, sticky blood covered Admar's hands and knees where he crouched atop the man. His final breaths heaved weakly at Admar's bulk. Crescents of torchlight glimmered in the man's watery eyes as he stared up at his killer.

Admar felt no regret. Not for a damn snake. For Lakka and Ayra and Vanique and Barnhol, yes. For all those who wouldn't get to see justice done. The man before him had watched too many die at his feet for Admar to feel remorse in killing him.

No. Admar felt right, righteous even, as he dragged his weapon around the man's throat, then spat into the corpse's face. *That's two to prove my harmlessness.*

His chest heaved as he stood, yet the fluid pumping through his body had given him a burning strength. There was a smoothness to his movement now where fear had made him stiff before. The pain in his knee was forgotten.

He walked to the door the Scoth was guarding. He pulled it open a foot, well-oiled hinges making no sound. A frightened whimper made him hesitate—the boy the guards had mentioned. An old woman's giggle haunted the air.

Admar wasted no time. Not a second more of abuse would pass under his watch. Iron handle in his palm, he swung the door open and sprang through.

A boy cowered in the corner, crumpled sheets wrapped around his waist in an otherwise empty bed. A handful of torches adorned the walls. Admar cursed and swept the room. The apartments were bare and unoccupied. He looked at the boy again. "Where is she?"

The boy's eyes flickered. Dread propped up the hairs on the back of Admar's neck...

He whirled around just as the door slammed shut. "Two beauties. Now that's enough to make an old lady blush."

From behind the door, Carbuncle watched Admar with the confidence of a cat approaching cornered prey. Wrinkled dugs stretched to either side of a sagging potbelly that covered her crotch save for a few strands of scraggly gray.

Naked but far from vulnerable, this woman carried neither shame nor fear.

Admar lunged, knife outstretched. "Die, you nasty bitch!"

Black smoke billowed into the space before the Ruptured. Laughter filled the room. Admar's knife hand entered the acrid cloud. White spots filled his vision as searing pain snaked up his elbow. He screamed and threw himself sideways, spinning away from the toxic vapor. His knife clattered to the floor as he fell and crimson smeared the carpet where his smoking hand landed.

Shouts echoed from the hallway beyond.

Sweat sheeted down Admar's face as he struggled to his feet, patches of flesh bubbling on his hand. He knew to touch it would bring greater agony still.

Carbuncle took a few jiggling steps to the door and paused. "Pity you're maimed. I have no use for crippled fools." She opened it.

Three Scoths entered. Deadly warning lined their faces and honeyed light flashed on their ax blades. They spread out, arraying themselves between Admar and the Ruptured. "Are you hurt, Mistress?"

He searched for an exit. Panicked, animal gulping started at the back of Admar's throat as he fought to keep calm.

"Am I hurt?" Carbuncle said with mock incredulity. "Only that you asked. Now out of my way!" She shoved through them, sallow flesh rippling with every step.

Admar fixated on a window, then his gaze wandered back to Carbuncle who seemed to catch his intent.

"You could, but it's a hundred-foot fall to meet the stones." She clapped her palms together. "Ends with a crunchy little splat."

Admar stepped sideways. Blood ran in rivulets from the fingertips of his tattered hand. Flame chewed under the dead skin and sent a sharp throbbing all the way up to his shoulder. The pain was all-consuming, a demon's maw gnawing off his arm. If he jumped, his last thoughts would be of pain. *At least after, I'll be done with it forever.*

"Stay and you'll live."

Admar blinked at the hag.

"Your spirit's a bit too strong to let you die now," she said. "You must learn to respect your race's inferiority. You need...education. And I know just the place for it."

"The quarries," Admar said.

She nodded.

"Mistress is that—"

"My fucking desire? Why yes, it is!" She rounded on one of the soldiers. "Wise? Pfah. That's what you were going to say, wasn't it?" She rapped his helmet with a knuckle. The tendons in the man's jaw jumped, brow knitting together with obvious displeasure. "You're about as wise as they get, aren't you? Questioning me...because I'm a woman? Maybe you'd be wiser if I boiled your cock off, eh?"

The man shook his head and buried his defiant gaze into the floor. Carbuncle affected a courteous smile as she twirled back to face Admar, exceedingly more grotesque in her attempt to seem elegant.

"So...the slave quarries."

The slave quarries. Where Kanians and Kurgs and any criminal lucky enough to avoid immediate execution for their petty crimes labored until their deaths.

Admar glanced at the window. He'd have to squeeze through but he could make it if he tried. A gust of wind moaned through the opening. Heat licked the back of his neck. He craned around. *The torch. I could keep fighting. Perhaps take one of them with me to the grave.*

"If you want to jump out the window, I'll let you. Just choose quickly." Carbuncle glanced at the boy on the bed. "I have things to do."

Bile threatened, one part pain and the sight of his maimed hand, another the woman's predilections. He ground his teeth together. The abused boy was Lah-Tsarene, just like him. Once, it could have been him. *I'll show him what it is to fight. Show him that Scoths can be hurt. That freedom is worth dying for.*

Word might spread then. Someone, somewhere, might revolt.

Admar tried to determine which of the men holding axes was best to attack first but they were stone-still, not one betraying any signs of weakness.

"By the Sempyrean, he truly is stupid, isn't he?" Carbuncle picked at a grimy fingernail and then flicked white crud onto the carpet. "Take him."

Admar spun around to grab a torch, but something bashed into his heels. He pitched against the wall, hand groping empty air. Numbness splashed up his thighs as he landed hard on his knees. He twisted around onto his backside—the guards had kicked a stool across the room into his legs.

Now they were atop him.

The butts of their axes fell like rain, thudding down into his arms, his legs, his chest, numbing wherever they struck. "Enough!" Carbuncle shouted. The room spun. Hazy silhouettes crowded in. "Clean and bandage his hand. I want him healthy enough to go out with the next caravan. Wouldn't want him to die before he learns his lesson."

Admar's body unfurled across the cold floor. *I failed.* He laughed through bloody teeth. *Of course I did.*

Scothea did not lose. They never would.

Chapter Three

THE LUCKY ONES

Pain was the great preserver of life. With its hounding bite, Admar could not die. Obedience was the best way to avoid losing the next strip of flesh. That's how the Scoth slave masters did it. He wished nothing more than to relinquish his body and his life and all the horrors that accompanied them, but pain staked him through, imprinting itself in him. Fear of abuse drove his survival.

That was how a slave was made. And the Scoths were mighty skilled at it.

The lash had become a living and breathing part of Admar's environment, hedonistic in its tasting of his flesh. The others laboring in the yokes beside him had no fight left and gave no reaction as their backs were peeled one sting—one strip—at a time.

The captain of the guards was right. I am broken.

The wain he pulled groaned up a hill.

"Scrabble, mice!" shouted a guard.

Burning pain flashed across Admar's hip. The ache in his palms and the sting of splinters were welcome distractions that dampened the fire left by the blow. His bare feet dug at the earth. He pushed with all his might, hoping it would stay the next strike but always knowing it wouldn't. Ayra had died from such a lashing. He wondered if the Scothean who'd just struck him was the same one that killed his sister. Sadness welled where an urgent vengeance once lived.

We'll all die this way. Generations of mice fed to the snakes.

They had bandaged his burned hand, at least. It itched fiercely, but to his surprise, they seemed to have done a decent job. It was the only time in recollection he'd witnessed Scoths do any good, even if the act was meant to ensure he learned a lesson in inferiority.

An older man beside him stumbled. Admar risked a look backward. The Scoth sitting in the cab snapped his fingers at a hulking voar pacing alongside the lead wain of the slave caravan, then pointed at the fallen elder. Eight feet of lumbering, man-made monster snatched a woman from the wagon bed by the arm. She screamed as she was pulled onto the dirt road, screamed louder when he roughly tore her rope bonds from her wrists, leaving red welts and bloody patches. Then he half-walked, half-dragged her to the front.

Admar nodded at the man separating him from the downed elder. "Quickly, help him up." But the other man kept his vacant eyes on the ground, too afraid to act.

Meanwhile, the elder struggled to rise. "Please." He begged through dry lips. He sat back, a weathered hand shaking over his swollen ankle. "Please."

Footsteps thudded nearer. The voar's shadow fell over the yoked slaves. Python fingers wrapped around the old man's ankle. He cried out as he was jerked free from the yoke.

"I'll take that eye!"

Admar swung his face forward just in time. The driver's lash licked his shoulder, leaving a stinging cut.

The crying woman moved swiftly to replace the elder.

"Please!" the old man wailed.

Admar heard the voar's six-foot steel rod rise, felt the chill of its shadow pass over him before it fell with a soupy crack. It wouldn't be the first corpse with a crushed skull they passed on their way to the quarries at Unturrus.

Nor would it be the last they left.

To his credit, Admar didn't collapse like so many of the others when they finally reached the settlement at the base of Unturrus. Through the final day they had been driven without rest. Five more of their number, including the woman who'd replaced the elder, were left upon the King's Road to be plucked to the bone by scavengers.

They're the lucky ones. They won't have to live the nightmare any longer.

Unturrus loomed over the group. Admar cursed the legendary mountain for giving powers to Carbuncle. She should have been one of the countless many who died in the attempt. Ripped apart by demons, if the rumors were true. That would have sufficed. And if she had, he wouldn't be a slave. Lakka and Barnhold would still be alive.

The scholars were wrong. Unturrus didn't bestow gifts, it bestowed curses.

A minute of blissful rest came and went, and then they were being herded along. Admar had spent so long in the yoke, hunched forward with his knees bent, that his muscles were accustomed to the position they'd strained in for so long. Now, they screamed as he stood upright.

How long will I last? Such questions were not meant to be asked. The summer night was warm enough, yet a chill went through him as the answer came. *Your life ended when you arrived.*

Lashes sang, packing them tight into a shuffling mass and urging them into a pen between two squat wood buildings. Admar was never good at sums, but if he had to guess, the group of slaves had to number upwards of fifty, all of them wearing thin shifts of rough fabric.

A pale Scoth with a wispy white beard and a gold cape that marked him as an Imperator stood on a platform outside one of the buildings. After a moment spent staring down at the stinking herd, he raised a hand and signaled to a nearby voar. The hulking man-creature slammed a cloth-covered club against a hanging brass plate.

Admar's scabrous hands sped to cover his ears. He reeled. Faint squeals rose up from those crowding around him who were too slow to defend against the piercing sound. Once the tone faded, and the ringing stopped, the Imperator cleared his throat.

"The first time that sound wakes you from your sleep, your work begins. Important work. Work to be proud of. Without a wall around Unturrus, your..." His mouth twisted with disdain. "...*kind* might feel emboldened to find their way up its slopes and we simply can't have those unworthy of bearing Unturrus's gifts running amok."

Admar glanced at the mountain's peak—a silhouette among the clouds. If he could, he'd give it a try now. His lover, his friends, his family—all gone. Nothing left to lose.

If I get a chance, maybe...

"Besides, your peers at Sacred Hill and the other camps are working ever so diligently to see the wall complete. We can't let them show you up now, can we?" He smiled; a second later it slid from his face. "The second time you hear the gong, your work ceases and you will be returned to your sleeping post. Fail to comply with these simple parameters and...well..." The Scothean officer shrugged, gold-enameled pauldrons bobbing, and then pointed to a dark lane lined by torches on the other side of the building. He spoke with casual indifference as if he gave the same speech daily. "Look to your right as you take your place in the line."

Whips cracked near the back of the group, sending them scrambling in the direction the Imperator had pointed. Admar pressed his elbows out to the sides to keep from falling and being trampled. A few sharp cries told him one or two others weren't so lucky.

Iron stands, as tall as a man, bore torches to either side of a wide path. Though the Imperator had told them to look to their right, Admar immediately caught motion to his left. He shielded his eyes from the blazing light and peered into the dark.

There, in the shadows, a figure lay on its side and shivered. A thick beam of wood stretched along the lane at waist height. Stakes were driven through the post into the ground, spaced at intervals of roughly a dozen feet.

Between every stake, a set of shining eyes stared back at Admar. Their gazes were hard and distant. The desperation he now felt had become a long-buried memory to them. All were seated or lying down, the chain linking them to the wooden beam no longer than the length of their bodies and attached by way of a manacle at the ankle.

More like animals than people.

An older boy was pulled from the slave herd with a yelp and escorted to the first empty shackle they passed. A moment later, he was locked into it. The Scoth guards kept the group moving forward, pulling individuals from the group to fill in the empty manacles as needed.

They passed hundreds of slaves, some sleeping and the rest disinterested in their new batch of forsaken peers. After forty minutes of walking, Admar was the last one left. The lane and its torches came to an abrupt stop. A Scoth at Admar's shoulder shoved him left.

A Kurgish woman sat up to watch as he was chained up beside her. Her eyes kept flickering past him, past the torchlight where the beam seemed to come to an end. She scratched her face—pinky, thumb, and forefinger were all that remained on the hand.

"You're an unlucky bastard." A Scoth clapped the lock on the manacle together, then turned a key inside it with a click. "The ones on the end survive longest. Better to die quick."

Without another word, he left. Admar took a few steps and the chain went taut, metal digging into his ankle bone. He winced and gingerly limped back a step.

"Lay down," the Kurgish woman said. "Save your strength. The first day will be a shock."

From the look of her, she'd managed to maintain some of her body weight whereas most of the others he'd seen were dangerously withered. Her golden skin shimmered under the torch's glow, lean muscle clinging to long limbs. She was Admar's height, maybe an inch taller, with a mane of lustrous black hair descending from a bulging forehead.

"What will happen?" His own voice was a stranger's. So meek.

The sound of metal slithering over turf came from the darkness at the end of the row. Admar spun about. A chain was attached to the beam, its length drawn tight into the murk of night. *Another slave? The guard said those on the end survive longest.*

The voice that greeted Admar from the darkness was anything but meek. Anything but hesitant. "You will see." The man's words punched the air with command.

Admar didn't respond. Instead, he lowered himself to the hard ground, plentiful with granite. After a minute, he could just make out the outline of a large man in the silvered moonlight. The only slave he'd seen standing.

Sleep tossed Admar about as if he traveled by ship on a troubled sea. Each slip into the depths brought him lurching back to the harrowing surface and waiting torment.

It wasn't until dawn that Admar remembered the words of the Imperator, or those of the slave at the end of the lane.

You will see...

It wasn't until dawn that he saw the endless gleaming of bones and rotting corpses filling the ditch on the other side of the lane.

Chapter Four

ANYWHERE BUT HERE

"Think of a time when you truly felt free."

Admar blinked at the towering man at the end of the line of slaves, his broad, muscular chest awash in the morning's glow.

"Think of your mother's smile. Her laughter." His words were aimed at Admar but he stood facing the lane with an unwavering expression. Of all the slaves Admar had seen, this man pinned back his shoulders and his granite chin did not dip in defeat.

He turned emerald eyes on Admar. "Think of anywhere but here. Think of a moment in the future when you are free." The man's voice fell low. "Where you feel proud. At peace."

They'd been standing over an hour since the crash of brass awoke them. A lot of time for Admar to consider the mounds of dead across the way.

A half-dozen voar had filed back and forth all morning wearing heavy, leather belts covered in iron loops. Guards had hurried to unlatch slaves from the sleeping posts and lock their chains to the voar's belts. Then they were escorted off to the quarries in batches of ten. If a voar wanted, they could brain most of those attached to them with a single sweep of their steel rod. If the slaves did ever manage to overwhelm one of the behemoths, they wouldn't get far locked to a quarter-ton carcass.

The man beside Admar continued. "Hold the image in your mind tighter than you would a weapon to protect your family. If your mind wanders to the atrocities around you, bring it to heel. Give it no purchase. Let nothing exist but what you dictate."

Admar turned to the man. His skin was smooth and boot-leather tan. "You're a Kanian."

"*The* Kanian," said the Kurgish woman. "He'll keep you alive here if you listen. So you best listen, Lah-Tsarene dog, or you will surely die."

Dark hair stirred over a shoulder as the big man's gaze swiveled slowly toward an approaching voar. "I take it you've never seen a Kanian before."

Admar shook his head. Scothea's invasion of the Fractured Lands had begun with the Desolation of Kania, a genocide for all but those who'd been enslaved.

"My people are reduced," he said. "Naught but meatless vessels and sightless eyes. They are hard to recognize, but I assure you, we are far from gone. The motherland still lives in them."

"You're so young," Admar said. "You must have been born into slavery then."

The Kanian raised an eyebrow. The Kurg cackled. He, the joke between the two.

It took Admar a moment to realize why. He looked down at the manacle clasped to his ankle. While the conditions were harsher in the slave quarries, little had changed from the life he'd had before. For anyone who wasn't a Scoth, birth in the Fractured Lands was a sentence passed, and the punishment was life without possibility.

Admar's eyes snapped up to meet the Kanian's. He found the man searching his face in turn. Assessing, judging, seeking the measure of him. *I am broken.*

Yet the Kanian's presence dredged hope to the surface once more. The final gasp of a notion he thought he had let die...not quite dead after all.

"Who are you?" Admar asked.

"Danath." He gestured at the Kurg. "Harcune. And that big voar is Glutton. Do not make eye contact with him. Do not do anything to draw his attention."

"Glutton?" Admar shifted his attention back to the slaver teams, and as he did, Harcune waggled her hand at him—two fingers missing.

"Oh." Admar shivered at the idea of having his fingers bitten off. The massive mutant they called Glutton was half a head taller than his brethren, and a good deal heavier. The iron rod he held was stained with rusty splotches. Like the other voar, Glutton had steel-capped teeth etched with runic symbols. Unlike the others, his teeth were filed to points.

"Remember," whispered Danath as a Scoth hustled toward them. "Think of anywhere but here."

One hundred and seven was not the number of days Admar had been at the quarries; it was a far crueler number.

The first day had been a shock, just as Harcune had suggested it would be. Admar's hands had bled, the skin of his palms shedding in opalescent patches like a snake's. By the time the gong sounded at day's end, he could barely move his shoulders.

What Harcune hadn't said was every day after the first wouldn't be any better. The physical demands of carting granite slabs all day were grueling, but the mental toll far outstripped the suffering of the flesh. To slow down was to be whipped by one of the guards or bludgeoned by one of the voar who haunted the pits among the slaves. Danath had told Admar to never let this happen. "Your mind can overcome the impulse to rest. Injuries are death in a place like this."

Admar had listened, and for his compliance, he'd worked himself to the bone. Some days he wished for nothing more than to falter and lie there until a voar crushed his skull.

Harcune's gentle barbs kept him going as much as Danath's encouragement. "Are all Lah-Tsarene dogs so weak? How did you ever push my people into the deep ranges?"

After a few weeks, Admar lost count of the days. It didn't matter anymore. The quarries were where he'd die. He observed time's passing by the number of dead now. That was something. To see another face in the ditch that was not his own meant everything. Stay alive, he told himself. Stay alive, Harcune and Danath echoed.

He did what he had to do. It brought him no great pleasure, but he found meaning in the deaths of his peers, and so it became less about days until he died and more about the others he'd outlived.

One hundred and seven dead mice.

Another day came to an end.

Hooked to their post for the night, they waited for the torches to be lit and the feeding crew to arrive. A pair of soldiers with a cart full of bread trundled by, tossing out hunks of salted bread and letting them drink their fill from buckets of warm water.

"Drink more than you can," Danath had said.

Admar listened. He choked down water until his belly was full, more still until it hurt.

For those with some muscle on their frame, a helping of fat and gristle was often plopped onto their bread. Admar devoured his, knowing the energy would keep him alive despite the snot-like texture. Those whose bodies were too slender discovered the hard way that Scothea was a culture built on efficiency. The guards did not waste resources on those they deemed unworthy of it.

"That's four today," Admar said as he and Harcune watched the feeding crew wave Glutton over to deal with a skeletal slave. The Scoths weren't wrong in their assessment. The slave lacked the energy to scream properly as the voar sauntered over and mushroomed their skull with a massive fist.

Harcune shook her head. "So little fight left in some of them."

"Only some?" Admar had meant to share the cynical joke, but his own half-hearted chuckle died in his throat. He cleared it. "Why haven't either of you tried to escape?"

Danath bit off a piece of bread, neck and jaw muscles flexing as he chewed and then swallowed. "I did. When I was young."

Warm summer wind tousled Admar's hair; it was getting longer, greasier, thinner. His body, too, was leaning out—he hadn't started with much meat on his frame to spare—but he doubted he'd be getting his skull caved in by Glutton any time soon.

"My mother was pregnant when she was taken to work in the house of a Scoth Imperator at Breckenbright," Danath said. "I was born there and trained as a scribe. When my mother died, I tried to escape but few boys of eleven are capable of such undertakings. As punishment, they sent me here."

Admar gaped. *Ten years...ten years of splitting stone without rest. No wonder he's so strong.*

"Though I was born into slavery, I've never once thought of myself as such." Danath's stare rose to take in Unturrus. "A free mind can never be bound by anything but that which it allows."

"You're well and chained up now. Just like the rest of us." Again, Admar's attempted humor was spared any laughter. He grumbled and followed Danath's gaze. Unturrus's peak split the sun, throwing shadows over the slave camp. "Do you think a slave could survive?"

"Anyone *can*." Harcune shrugged. "But few do."

The world is an unjust place. Because Carbuncle had survived, Lakka and Barnhold were gone. The horrible woman had been gifted powers for her gambit. All Admar had gotten for his own risk were shackles and slave labor for the rest of his life. *Wrong in every way, this world. When the Abyssal Sea rises up to take me, I won't be too sad to be rid of it.*

"I used to write notes for my former master while he read books, many of them about the Mountain of Power and its mysteries," Danath said. "I recall him saying that unity was the key to surviving it. One had to understand who they were and where they came from, a complete integration of past and present. Harmonious alignment. Otherwise, death." Danath paused, calm sliding over him, and yet, Admar sensed a subtle spark underneath it all. Something shifting within the Kanian—opening—an indecipherable gravity holding Admar in the man's thrall. "What my master failed to realize is that life beyond Unturrus's slopes is no different. Who can truly live but those willing to understand what they are, to defend the truth of their humanity at all costs?"

Admar swallowed, fear thickening in his throat.

Eyes narrowed, Danath looked to Harcune. "What is the Kurgish word for unity?"

Harcune's voice was hoarse. She, too, seemed to sense the tidal wave of Danath's purpose. "Namarr."

The Kanian nodded, then lay back in the grass. "If we had namarr, we would be free." He left the rest unsaid.

"What?" Admar said, but Danath rolled away from him, revealing a broad back, dense with scars. "Danath, what do you mean, 'free'?"

The Kanian never responded.

Sometime later, Harcune's whisper reached out in the night. "It's his dream."

"What is?"

"Danath. He dreams of freedom. He thinks if the slaves can come together they can—"

Admar hushed her to quiet. "Don't let anyone else hear you say that. They'll report you." Slaves turning in their peers for simple but brief comforts was not unheard of. *Just like in Brighthaven. Danath was right. The differences between citizens and slaves were minimal.* A bitter taste filled Admar's mouth. His warning to Harcune echoed the one Lakka had given him right before they'd killed her.

Maybe I should go to the Imperator. Turn Danath in. That's what Lakka should have done. If she had, maybe she would have lived.

Harcune seemed to sense his unease. "It is possible. That's all. There are four quarries like this one around Unturrus, each one with hundreds more slaves and too few masters."

Admar scoffed. "They have axes, armor—by the gods, they have voar."

Harcune sat up, face contorted, ready to let loose on Admar.

"It's not a matter of armor that keeps us weak." Admar's heart lurched as Danath came to stand behind him.

The Kanian experimentally tugged at the loops of chain anchoring him to the sleeping post. "And it isn't numbers that will give us a chance to succeed. You see, I have been trapped here for over a decade with little but my mind as my companion. I have had long nights and dark days, but I have also seen what *could* be." He pointed, silvery moonlight framing his finger as it jabbed at Unturrus. "There is no better example of the power of belief than that. And so, it is the mind—our idea of Scothean superiority—that keeps us weak. Every one of us looks into the eyes of their neighbor with a coward's hope that *they* have the answer. That someone else is strong enough. They take their hopes for a savior to their graves."

Danath jerked the chain taut, breaking the quiet of night.

Admar jolted and cast about, worried one of the voar who patrolled at night might hear.

Then the Kanian took a step toward him, demanding his attention, torchlight peeling back the dark, revealing granite features. He spoke low, his voice as resolute as iron. "No one looks to themselves for the answer. The day we see that inside ourselves is the day we start believing we have a chance. And that's day we walk the path of freedom. ."

"There is no chance." Admar shook his head as he recalled Barnhold's gritted teeth, his guts spilling onto his lap, and Lakka's corpse bursting apart and leaking over the floorboards like a rotten patch of melons. Fainter still, he recalled a prostrate and pale Vanique, shivering and begging him for more water, begging to make the burning stop. "I've seen what happens to those who stand up to Scothea. They have Awakened, Ruptured, voar...worse."

Danath jerked at the chain again. This time, the clamor sent a rustle of activity up the line of slaves as those startled awake moved around in the grass. Slow and deliberate, Danath eased himself to the turf. "Fear. It is the most effective weapon, isn't it? A snake has but one mouth to bite, but we, the mice, outnumber them a thousand to one. You think it so unbelievable for us to gnaw off the snake's head before we're all killed? The individual fears for its life and flees out of instinct. Isolated, we become prey. Operating as one though, as a single entity, we have a chance."

Admar scoffed. "They'd thresh us like wheat."

Danath crouched and gripped Admar's shoulder. While the touch was meant to be gentle, he couldn't help but feel the unyielding power there. "You're no fool, Admar. Just imagine it. That's all I ask."

Chapter Five

RUDE AWAKENINGS

- SUMMER, YEAR 522 A.R. -

Two hundred dead marked the elapsed time of Admar's enslavement. Just as many came to replace the ones that died—a never-ending supply. Their deaths were a necessary pittance sacrificed to New Scothea's grand vision of swaddling Unturrus with a curtain wall. They wanted the Mountain of Power protected, controlled, for the economic might its psychoactive plants would bring, and its supply of Ruptured and Awakened as well. The jewel of the world some called it.

Someday, Scothea would own the world. Someday, they would possess it all.

And they'll step on my back to get there.

After Danath's offering, Admar had pulled away from both he and Harcune. They reminded him too much of Barnhold and Lakka, and he'd seen firsthand where they'd ended up. It brought him little pleasure to avoid his closest companions in the slave camp, yet it was necessary.

Every morning, when they were hooked to Glutton's vest of iron rungs, Admar refused to make eye contact with either of his friends. Today was no different.

Danath guided another slave out of the way and positioned himself beside Admar, then risked a low spoken word. "Look and see." He gestured with his chin ahead of them, at the dozens of slaves chained to lumbering voar. Hundreds more could be heard from down in the quarry already, picks ringing. *The number of guards compared to slaves, that's what he wants me to see.*

"I'm already a slave to one master." Admar shrugged off the bigger man's dark hand. "I won't have you be a second." He stepped over a chain, putting another slave between Danath and himself.

Glutton's pockmarked visage swung about, bovine-slow and blank of expression. He growled then jerked Admar's chain, propelling him onto his knees in the dirt. The voar blotted the sun as he stepped to within striking distance.

Danath's smaller silhouette stepped to meet him. He whistled, acting ignorant of the exchange. The voar grunted and shoved the Kanian back a step; such a push would have thrown anyone else to their backside.

Danath stooped as the group started forward. "You have to see, brother."

The muscles in Admar's jaw tightened. He ignored Danath's outstretched hand and scrambled after the group before his chain started to drag him. Danath stalked at the rear. More than a few of the other slaves glanced back. The haunted look was still there, but so was something else. Curiosity, perhaps. Their gaze seemed to flit back and forth between Admar and Danath as if trying to solve a puzzle.

They filed down a switchbacking path, trodden smooth over time but for a handful of jutting rocks.

At the bottom, a pair of guards assigned tools to the slaves, then sent them to their places. Danath, Harcune, and a handful of others broke boulders into manageable chunks, while the rest of the slaves were tasked with loading them out of the quarry onto carts at ground level. From there, they'd be processed into cut stone at another slave camp closer to Unturrus.

Work went at a frenetic, mind-numbing pace. Thinking slid into the hands and feet, emptied into labored breaths. Whips snapped in rhythm against air and flesh, the intervals of some dread clock. Rock tumbled, forming skirts around the mounds of the rock crushers.

Harcune and Danath's picks bit through stone while Admar scrambled to load granite to the liking of patrolling voar.

Midday came and went in a nightmarish blur.

Reprieve came in the form of buckets of tepid water and a five-minute break. "Six ladles each!" a guard bellowed.

Harcune sidled up to Admar, wearing a smirk. Glistening beads raced down her cheeks from the front half of her bare skull. Her dark, lustrous hair was damp, her lean shoulder muscles swollen with blood. Like most Kurgish females, she was tall—taller than Admar even, and he was no short man.

"Still living blind are you, Lah-Tsarene?" She took the water bucket, withdrew the ladle, and drank.

Admar didn't respond. He knew what she wanted. *I've been down that road before and it landed me here.* Nothing scared him more than discovering what might befall him next if he gave Danath and Harcune what they wanted. "I wasn't done yet."

"What a mighty bark from such a pathetic dog." She drank more. The ladle paused at her lips. She glanced to either side. No guards were near. The confrontational air left her, replaced by a sheath of calm. "One should not unsee the truth, brother."

He turned to go but she grabbed his hand. "You look but you do not see."

"Let go." She didn't. He pulled harder, but her grip was unbreakable after so many days swinging the pick. "I'm not your brother."

"But you are," she hissed. "We have no choice but to be as *one*, the many parts of a fractured people. You think you are too weak, too scared, but in truth, the only thing you lack is faith. *We* are strong. That means you are too."

"Slave!" A dozen paces off, a guard squared to them. "Back to work!"

Harcune grimaced but kept his hand gripped tight. "When you look at *them*, what do you see within yourself?"

Admar hesitated. The guard had unfurled his whip and now strode in their direction. *I see what I always see.* He saw himself stretched out on a table, cowering, while Scothean troops lorded over the bodies of his murdered friends nearby. *This one is broken.*

"I see failure."

Harcune released his hand and straightened. "That is because you think yourself alone. You are not. *We* are here, brother."

Leather split the air over Harcune's back. She yelped and dropped the bucket. Water splashed the dusty earth.

"Get back to work!" The guard sent her running for her pick with a second blow, though it fell short.

The guard turned to deal Admar a similar punishment, but he was already gone. He cursed himself for sneaking away like a frightened mouse. A part of him wished to share the lash with Harcune, to stand defiantly by her side, swathed in dreams of freedom, ready to bear whatever cruelty the Scoths had to give.

Not far off, Danath stood ringed by a handful of slaves. He seemed to be whispering to them as he worked, a brazen act with a Scoth guard so close.

Maybe it is possible. A swell of desperation within wanted to believe. The urgency of it clawed upward. The rage of injustice soared louder with each second that he failed to quash the dangerous ideal.

But he'd been hollow too long.

Danath's dream echoed through him like a drumbeat in the deep.

Screams brought Admar awake, a bucket of icy, cruel reality dousing him.

At first, he thought it was another nightmare of his own making, but then he saw a heavyset man punching Glutton's root-thick arms.

"Hid a file in his arse," said the man on the other side of Harcune. Word carried up and down the slave line quickly. "Caught by a guard with a partially shaved manacle."

The gloom before dawn gave the unfolding scene a dreamlike quality.

The man fighting Glutton was nearly as tall as Danath, though twice as thick through the middle. Compared to a voar, his size helped him little. He may as well have been a child.

Three feet taller, and twice as heavy, Glutton dealt the man a slap that dropped him to a knee. Then the voar grabbed him by the ankle and lifted him into the air to dangle upside down. Rope-like tendons and slabs of muscle twitched across the voar's back as he yanked the slave's ankle free from the manacle with a sickening pop. Scarlet sprayed across Glutton's face. The man in the voar's grasp went pale, eyes lolling at the sudden loss of blood.

The Imperator strode down the lane, his gold cloak stirring the dust in his wake. His wispy, white beard tuft was dragged back along his jawline by the wind. "I'll have the two beside him as well." A young boy, no more than thirteen, and an older woman.

Guards complied with mechanical efficiency. A half minute later, the man whose foot had been flayed by his own manacle lay bleeding and whimpering in the dirt and the woman and boy were thrown down to either side of him.

"Any rumbling of insurrection must be reported," the Imperator announced. "Scheming will not be met with tolerance. Anyone who does not report their neighbor will be seen as a conspirator and duly punished." He gestured with an upturned palm at the line of slaves, and then back to the three who'd been plucked from them. "Witness."

Spade-broad hands snaked around the boy's neck. Doe-eyes bulged as Glutton lifted him squirming, feet kicking puffs of dust. Small, weak hands clawed at the giant's grip. Futile.

"Scoths are not people," said Harcune.

Admar looked away.

A sharp crack was followed by a heavy thud and the clatter of bones as the boy was tossed into the ditch across the way. *Two hundred and one...*

"Look," Danath said, his tone urgent. "See."

The woman shrieked. Another crack, thud, and clatter. *Two hundred and two...*

"You must look. Fear turns you away." Danath risked taking a few steps closer to Admar. The motion went unseen as all eyes were fixed on the executions in the lane. Danath brought his mouth close to Admar's ear and whispered. "There is no savior. See what happens with your heart and soul."

Admar inhaled sharply, then turned to watch.

The heavyset man blubbered as Glutton hauled him upright. All his weight leaned on his uninjured leg. The other was dark with blood that pooled underfoot. Glutton grabbed the man by the neck and shoulder, holding him still. He reared back then brought his ugly maw crashing into the side of the man's throat. The voar jerked back, mouth filled with glistening wet flesh. The man trembled violently as ichor sluiced down his bare chest. He touched a hand to the side of his tattered neck for the briefest of seconds before it flopped back down at his side. He swooned and toppled face-first in a heap.

Glutton swung the dead body by the leg and sent it skidding into the ditch with the rest. *Two hundred and three.*

Danath's dream shattered before Admar's eyes. "I see." Fear coiled around his heart, squirming prey already in the viper's jaws. "I see three people who could still be alive if they weren't fools."

A solemn expression darkened Danath's face, and for a moment, Admar wasn't sure who he should fear more: the Scoths or the Kanian.

Chapter Six

THE SHADOWS OF MEN

I t was the peak of summer and Admar toiled under the hammering sun. He glanced over his shoulder. Mounds of rock and a flurry of bobbing heads separated him from Danath and Harcune.

Two score guards ringed the quarry, the majority of those stationed at the camp. A handful of voar patrolled the rock-strewn grounds, grunting displeasure at every turn.

Admar's gaze settled on Danath. Tan skin gleamed with sweat and whipcord muscle twitched with every swing of the pick. After ten years of the same grueling work, the Kanian had come to resemble the rock he now hewed. He was a restless inferno. There were no benefits to out-producing his peers, yet he was unceasing in his drive. Admar frowned as he watched the man perform his frenzied task. *Perhaps he's gone insane.* Slavery had a way of twisting the mind, Harcune had told him. Admar wondered if her friend had fallen victim to her notion without her realizing it.

Admar sighed and bent to roll a hunk of jagged granite onto a hide gurney. He was tired of seeing new faces, only to have them staring up from the ditch a few days later with vacant expressions. He was tired of the past, the way it pinched at the nape of his neck every time he thought the word, 'friend'. The ax still hung there, tickling the back of his head, waiting, begging him to test its edge and stand defiantly. But he'd grown comfortable lying down, knowing that if he did not act, he would not die.

I'm tired of hope. Hope killed his friends. It made a joke of justice. Hope broke a man's spirit better than any Scoth ever could. And unless he let it go, he would never be free of the festering at the core of him that rose up to coat his throat every time he saw his brutalized hands. Yet here he was, having it shoved in his face at every turn by Danath and his foolish beliefs.

Hope...it weighed more on his soul than every stone in the quarry combined.

"Quick." The woman he'd been partnered with for the day scooped to the ground to help him to roll granite onto the gurney at Admar's feet. "Don't be caught dawdlin'."

He took up the poles at the rear while she took the ones at the front. Together they lifted it and then made their way up the switchbacking incline to the carts.

The sun beat down. They'd already had their midday water break; it would be hours before the next. The sweat on Admar's shoulders was all that cooled him. Almost, he appreciated the work for that bit, like drinking a poison that was his only antidote.

A guard's face swung toward Admar—he looked down, adjusted his grip. He heard the woman shuffle to one side, thrown off balance by Admar's movement. "You're bouncing it."

The guard took a step onto the lane, hand drifting to the leather-bound handle of his lash.

Fuck. Admar pursed his lips.

"Too slow!"

He winced at the words, knowing what trailed them.

The whip raked his ankle, leaving a burning gash. Admar gritted his teeth and hobbled onward, each step shooting pain up into his calf. Behind him, the woman whispered not to drop it.

He breathed in deeply, wishing to be anywhere else. His mother peered at him from murky memory, a homely woman with lined pockets of flesh around her eyes. Danath had said to imagine her smiling or laughing, but she never did any of that. She had always just watched the Scoth soldiers pass by stoically before looking at her children with eyes devoid of hope. That's how it had been and that's how it was now.

An unsmiling past reflected in a joyless future.

Danath couldn't know the truth. He'd been a slave all his life. How could he know there was nothing left beyond the slave camps? *I'm not broken. The people of the Fractured Lands are.*

"Three, two..."

They dumped their load and then descended the trail into the quarries. The wound in Admar's ankle left a trail of dark, speckled beads in the dust. He didn't let it slow him though, and avoided eye contact with the guard who'd punished him.

The woman guided the hide gurney over to where Danath labored.

Chest heaving, the Kanian split a boulder in two, then stood upright. Veins arced up his forearms and into his hand wrapped around the handle of the pick. *After ten years, the man's grip must be like iron. If he wanted, he could strangle me in my sleep with ease.*

Admar hunched over and looked down. He didn't want to end up like the three Glutton had killed. Better to divest himself from Danath in every way or it would be his throat torn out.

Face downcast, he bent to his work, praying to hear the sound of the pick resume, the sound of a preoccupied Danath. When he didn't, his heartbeat quickened, and he knew the man watched him.

As he bent to retrieve another stone, Admar risked a glance upward. His stomach lurched. Emerald eyes bore down on him from Danath's heavily silhouetted face. A moment of passing scrutiny ended with a subtle nod to Admar, neither friendly nor condemning. The uncertainty of it spiked fear through his chest. *Does he still seek to win me over? Or does he sense the betrayal rolling through my mind?*

Eager to be out from under Danath's judging eye, Admar rushed to lift a stone and fumbled it.

"Don't rush," the woman said.

Pick rang against rock as Danath set back to work. Relief washed over Admar as he secured a stone on the gurney and then gripped the handles. His partner was slow to take up her own. Admar threw furtive looks back at Danath.

The Kanian's pick punched through rock—punched through again, each successive strike falling quicker than the last. Admar felt the building anger in every reverberation. Rage mounting... *He knows. He knows.* Danger was supposed to lurk in the master's shadow, not a friend's. The traitorous nature of soured camaraderie added an extra layer of panic. *I'll ask to be moved tonight. Maybe tell them what he said...*

The woman groaned as she lifted her handles. She spoke low. "A bit heavy in'it?"

"Just go," Admar hissed.

He threw a look over his shoulder at Danath just as the man sundered a boulder in two with a thunderous blow.

Admar shuffled forward—something slammed into his toes. He hurtled forward, gurney handles ripped from his hands. He pitched to one side, landed in the dust, and rolled. A handful of upthrust rocks dug at his flesh as he came to a stop on his stomach.

The flurry of activity in the pit slowed to a drip. Aching pain seeped into Admar's knee, side, and shoulder, numbing rapidly like he'd been kicked by a horse.

Booted feet closed with him as he struggled to his feet.

A Scoth drew out a loop of whip and let it unfurl to the ground with a soft thud.

"Please, I—" Admar stopped, cursing himself for words he knew would lead him nowhere.

The Scoth brought the leather tip of his lash backward, his other hand stretching forward for balance.

Admar twisted away, cowering. He'd seen slaves who didn't turn quick enough. The Scoths were good. Usually, it cost the slave an eye or ear, or in the worst scenario, a testicle.

A shadow fell over Admar. A voar come to break him in two, no doubt. Powerful arms wrapped around his torso, a broad, sweat-damp chest pressing against his back. Admar expected the breath to be crushed out of him any second. He thrashed, fighting for escape. But he was held fast, a toddler in their father's embrace.

The crack of the whip, the absence of its sting, the jolt of the body atop him—all of it brought Admar to stillness. The arms had not tightened, though they held him firmly in place. Confusion sapped Admar's frenzied urge to flee.

"Ha!" The Scoth guard laughed meanly. "You'll take thrice as many for your lover then."

Calm and resolute, Danath spoke in his ear. "Do you see now?"

The whip sang. Admar felt pain shudder through Danath's body pressed against his own.

"This is our strength."

Another snap of the lash.

"*This* is unity."

Three more strikes came in rapid succession, and with each, Danath grunted, unwilling to release his hold.

"This." Danath's voice was strained. "This is namarr."

"Enough!" Another Scoth said. "Hurt the big one too bad and it'll slow production."

Danath let go. Admar stumbled a few steps then turned to watch the bigger slave sway, seemingly light-headed, then walk back to his place atop a mound without another word. His back bore Admar's mistakes in bloody writing—that said enough.

"Next time, you both die." A guard shoved Admar toward the gurney. "Back to your place!"

"He's insane," Admar muttered.

Ten years. No slave lived that long. Not with their mind intact, anyway. *Is he delusional, seeing possibility where none exists?*

Admar picked up his end of the gurney and found Harcune watching him from a mound, her face a craggy, unreadable mask. She tilted her broad forehead toward him, then swung her pick overhead.

She, too, was strong. None believed in Danath more than she. *Maybe I'm the one who's lost his mind...because I've given up.*

Something had to be done. Someone had to put a stop to the madness, if not for himself, then for those like Harcune who clung to hope.

CHAPTER SEVEN

BROKEN

"**S**tand here." The Scoth tugged at Admar's chain and pointed at the floor, a master directing a dog. "Wait." He leaned forward to bang on a door, then whispered against it when a gruff answer came.

Admar afforded a brief look at his surroundings. Carved over the door was a depiction of Jathos Wrathhand, conqueror of the Fractured Lands and destroyer of Kania. Other Scoth kings of lesser importance spread to either side along the wall, each smaller than the last until the carvings met floorboards.

The guard pursed his lips and threw a deadly look at Admar. He shied away to stare out the window at the end of the long hall.

Outside, guards huddled around stumps playing games while a clutch of voar devoured the carcass of a bull on the steps of the barracks.

"Enter." The Imperator's voice frayed at Admar's resolve.

No turning back. The guard hauled Admar within by the elbow.

The Imperator's office was simpler than expected, nowhere near the opulence of Carbuncle's apartment at the keep of Brighthaven. If Admar had to guess, the post of running a slave camp across the ocean wasn't ideal for a Scothean politician scraping his way to power at the top of the shit heap. Chances were, the Imperator had crossed the wrong man, and given his stuffy demeanor and a relish for spite, Admar imagined it wouldn't have taken much.

Candles had dissolved into skirted puddles of fat at the corners of his desk, deepening the shadowed recesses of his heavily lined face. He perused a glowing piece of parchment as he smoothed his wispy white beard. Despite the late hour, he still wore armor over a velvet tunic. Breeches lined with fox fur descended into his boots.

No wonder the Scoths conquered the Fractured Lands. They never stop working. Historians called the inexorable expansion through war and economic efficiency the 'Scothean juggernaut,' a cultural ideal that crushed all in its path.

How could Danath think they had a chance to defeat a machine that never rested? A dart of guilt sank into Admar's gut. *Traitor...*

He gulped but the knot in his throat remained. *I must play the part.* He summoned what courage he could and stretched himself taller. It wasn't just his life at stake. Hard as it was, Harcune and the others needed him to do this.

"Why?" The Imperator drew out the word, more accusation than question. A second later, head unmoving, he turned hard eyes up at his subordinate.

The guard prodded Admar. "Speak."

Self-preservation. That was all that mattered now. "One of the slaves is plotting a rebellion, Master."

Faint laughter filtered through the window from the barracks, into the otherwise silent room.

The Imperator's cheek twitched into a half-smile. He blinked then leaned back. "Really? And I suppose you think by sacrificing your fellow slave that you'll get some special treatment?"

A prayer to the Sempyrean bubbled through Admar, more of a feeling than specific words. "No. I just—I just wanted you to know, Master. No one needs to die."

I've seen enough of that. Vanique's waxen face as she died, Barnhold's severed head rocking on the floor, and Lakka's ruined flesh—the image of a hundred other strangers' glazed-over eyes staring up into the Abyssal Sea—flashed before his mind's eye.

All just bones on display now.

"Well, at least *one* surely does." With a self-satisfied chuckle, the Imperator stood and reached for an arkiev—a long, curved officer's dagger—resting on a hook behind him, then buckled it around his waist. "We haven't had a slave with such gall in some time. It only seems fitting that I discuss his plans with him."

The Scoth guard shoved Admar into the hall. "Lead."

Still injured from his foot wound earlier in the week, he hobbled down the steps of the administrative building and into the slave pen. From toe to heel, the pain throbbed all the way into the knee, but he smothered the feeling and made his way quickly.

A trio of drunk Scoths stood in a triangle casting coins into the dirt and playing sachari as Admar shuffled past with the Imperator in tow. One of the guards balanced a small leather sack filled with rice on his ax blade before spinning the handle and flinging it into the air. Just as one of the others lunged forward to catch the sachari on his own blade, the guard flanking Admar cleared his throat with urgency. The sachari plopped into the dirt, and the three guards spun about to salute the Imperator as he swept past. Lucky for them, their leader had a more urgent mission and strode down into the dead of night, ignoring them.

Torches guttered along the slave lane, flames whipping sideways from their poles with every hot gust of wind like lecherous tongues searching for a taste of violence. Admar shivered. *You'll get it soon enough.*

The bones of the dead glimmered to Admar's right; a caved-in skull, a shattered ribcage, a cleave wound running down pelvis and thigh. Countless thousands lay in that ditch. Admar wondered if, by night's end, he would finally rest among them.

"Where?" The Imperator kicked him in the backside, causing him to yelp and stumble.

Admar clenched his teeth and mumbled. "The end, Master."

In cheery tones, the Imperator said, "Proceed, then. I expect to be done with this before dawn."

It was a few hundred yards to Danath. *It will all be over soon.* Admar pushed on, a pinch in his tailbone with every step now.

A pale face intersecting mountainous shoulders materialized from the darkness to their left.

The Imperator cursed and lurched back a step. He wasn't used to seeing Glutton in the night like Admar was. "What are you doing out here?"

The voar grunted, massive torso convulsing around the sound.

The guard spoke for the eight-foot savage. "He's on patrol, my Lord." Voar's tongues were removed as infants, giving them the ability to take orders but never give them. Word had it, there had been an uprising in the earliest years of the breeding pits.

"Well." The Imperator snorted. "He reeks of impropriety. Savaging slaves in the dark, I assume. A direct violation of Ghulkov's Edict of Conduct. We do not intermix pure blood with that of vermin. Half rations for a week."

Glutton's chin dipped like a reprimanded child, face slack with disappointment. The rune-etched, metal teeth of his lower jaw shimmered in the torchlight, reminding Admar not to feel sorry for the monster no matter how pathetic he now looked.

The Imperator jabbed Admar in the ribs and spoke over a shoulder to the voar. "Follow. You shall do the holding while I do the carving."

While the guard and Imperator seemed content to flank Admar, Glutton's thumping steps brought up the rear, the tip of his steel rod dragging through the dirt with a rustling ring—the terror of any slave.

But as they went, brazen whispers floated in the dark, traveling up and down the slave line. "He broke them."

Feeling leaked from Admar's legs. *He couldn't have.* Like any slave, he'd tested the chains before, many times. To all but maybe a voar, breaking them was impossible.

"The Kanian..." they said in hushed tones. "He broke his chains."

The Imperator scoffed.

Most of the slaves were awake now and shuffled between their neighbors to spread the impossible words. A dozen paces farther and the whispers were abandoned in favor of excited chatter.

"He broke them—"

"Broke his chains."

"Who did?"

"The Kanian."

"The Kanian?"

"...the Kanian."

Danath.

The Imperator stopped and whirled toward the line of slaves. "Silence! Or the next of you who makes a sound will answer to him." He motioned with his chin at Glutton. The voar grinned and gnashed sharpened, stained teeth.

"All the way to the end, is it?" The Imperator's tone was impatient.

Admar pointed ahead. "Just there, Master."

The Imperator looked back down the line. A sea of haunted eyes watched them, waiting for the desperate gossip to be confirmed.

Dread clawed at Admar's insides, the distance to the end winnowing too fast for comfort. *If we arrive and Danath is gone, will they kill me on the spot?* He decided it didn't matter. He'd made his gamble. *One way or another, I won't survive the week.*

Admar angled down into the ditch. His own chains were empty. Harcune stood on the other side of the post, as far from Glutton as she could.

It took a moment for their eyes to adjust. When they did, Admar's insides froze.

Danath's chain was clasped to the pole. But Danath was gone. The guard swiped his foot through the ankle-high grass in wide, slow arcs. He struck something, lowered himself into a crouch, then raised the missing half of sundered chain.

One of the links was mangled and snapped open.

Admar's heart pounded. *Sempyrean save us, he's actually done it.* A cascade of emotions tingled under his skin. Pride gave way to rage, a rage long concealed, long imprisoned. He wanted to weep, to scream, to hide from what came next. To kill and feel the flesh of the enemy under his nails.

But fear trapped it all in place, a breath trapped in his chest. Admar waited, pulse crashing in his ears. He'd done his part.

Now it was time for Danath to do his.

"Impossible," the Imperator sneered. "Someone let a tool go missing. They will be punished for this."

"It is you who will be punished, Imperator." Prickles swept up the back of Admar's neck as Danath's voice echoed from the darkness, booming with fearless bravado.

The guard rose, ax looping up over his shoulder in both hands. The Imperator whipped toward the darkness hanging over the ditch of bones, eyes wild, cheek twitching. "Come then, *slave*." He laughed. "Come out of the dark to punish me."

A gloved hand snaked out, fingers twining through a handful of Admar's hair. The Imperator twisted. Searing pain swallowed the back of Admar's head. With Glutton in tow, the Imperator dragged him onto the road between the rows of torchlight. "Come out now, or for every minute you delay, I'll feed one of your brethren to my knife."

The arkiev pressed up under Admar's chin, cold to the touch. The Imperator's rabid face filled Admar's periphery. The man peered into the dark.

"My brethren are ready to die," Danath intoned. "Look for yourself. See the truth of your undoing."

"Where is he?" the Imperator hissed, breath reeking of yeast and acidity. The guard beckoned him to look down the line. He swiveled, Admar still in hand.

Every slave was standing, watching them, their chains slung through their palms. Waiting.

"I wanted them to see," Danath said. "I wanted them to know that, you, too, can be afraid."

The Imperator huddled in closer behind Admar. *You cannot hide. Not now. We have you*. Danath continued. "You're not welcome here, Scoth. These lands belong to us. We, the mice, have tolerated you long enough."

The arkiev floated from Admar's throat to the Imperator's side as he spat. "I'll flay you mysel—"

"Namarr!" Danath's thundering command dashed the Scoth's threat.

A thousand slaves heaved against their bonds. A thousand chains clanking together in a deafening clamor.

"Namarr!"

The legion of chains jerked taut again. The slave post creaked under the strain.

The Imperator jabbed his arkiev at the trench where the bones of three decades of slaves decomposed. "Find him!" He shoved Admar to the ground—a nothingness forgotten.

The guard charged off. The Imperator gestured at Glutton then swept his arm in an arc. "Kill them all!"

Glutton's steel rod stirred the night air with a heavy whoosh as he lurched toward the slave line. A heartbeat later, there was a scream and a sickening splat.

"Namarr!" The sleeping post swayed. Dirt pushed up at either side of the deep-driven stakes.

Admar scrambled to his feet. He plucked a torch from an iron pole. "Burn, snake!" The Imperator's stoic mask broke as he rounded, wide eyes illuminated in shock as Admar plunged the torch into his face. Embers burst around the filthy fucking Scoth's head. Impact jolted up Admar's arm.

The Imperator stumbled back, slapping at the flames and shrieking, but Admar flowed with him, eager to roast the bastard's flesh for as long as he could. The Scoth finally launched himself away, smoke trailing him into the shadows from tiny sprouts of fire in his beard.

Curses and the sound of struggle echoed from the darkness surrounding the bone ditch. *If the guard kills Danath, it's over.* Admar held little faith that their rebellion could succeed without the Kanian.

He broke his chains...

A gurgle stopped Admar at the edge of the ditch. *Gods, no.* He stepped back, expecting the guard to emerge any second and claim his head. He adjusted his grip on the torch, preparing to fight for his life.

Instead of the guard, Danath burst into the lane, chest splashed with blood, Scoth ax in hand. "They come, brother!" He pointed in the direction of the administrative buildings in the distance where cries of alarm were going up.

Before Admar could respond, his leader was off and running. He followed in the Kanian's wake, far slower with his mangled foot. Torches guttered low in the moaning wind but he could still make out the flurry of motion along the slave post where his brothers and sisters continued heaving in unison. Now damp, white wood peeked from the base of a few stakes driven shallower than the rest.

Glutton had descended on Harcune. Chained, weaponless, outmatched in every way, she was doing her best to dodge the voar, but anyone could see that a matter of seconds separated her from death.

The voar's six-foot rod thudded into the turf where Harcune had been a moment before. She scrabbled backward, slipping under the slave beam just in time to avoid having her head flattened by a second blow that landed against the sleeping post. The reverberation warbled in Admar's ear.

Danath hurtled toward Glutton. For a moment it looked as though he might catch the voar unaware, but Glutton spun around to face the slave leader's onslaught with ample time to react. The breath rushed out of Admar. The element of surprise was lost. Glutton grinned and raised his rod. The rebellion would die before it ever truly started.

Darkness consumed the distance between voar and slave-leader until naught but muscle and hate remained.

Despair poured down Admar's throat into his gut as Danath's warcry split the night. "Namarr!" A dying breath. A martyr's final gasp. The whoosh of the executioner's falling ax.

Death whistled toward Danath in a flat arc. If he were to duck or leap to one side and roll, there could have been a chance to survive. He did neither.

He stood fast. A silhouette of iron. A beacon of freedom and light.

Sparks exploded from Danath's ax as he looped it up and around and sent Glutton's rod flying over the top of him. The added momentum of the deflection turned the voar's shoulders halfway around, off-balancing him and exposing his side.

With the casual grace and speed of a mountain lion, Danath stalked forward to hew the monster's arm off at the elbow. Jets of dark blood shot across the grass. Glutton blinked dumbly at Danath, then at his glistening stump. The voar staggered back, its remaining hand groping for balance against the slave post.

Danath roared then dashed forth to lop the stunned mutant's head off with a resounding *thack*.

Like Admar, the other slaves had taken pause to gawk at the unfolding scene—illusions of impossibility shattered.

A single slave had broken his chains. A single slave had slain a voar.

A single slave had become his own master.

"Namarr!" Admar bellowed.

The slaves seemed to wake from their dreams. With renewed vigor, they hauled on their chains. Wood groaned, shrieked, splintered.

Admar inhaled sharply to loose another command, but it died in his chest as agony lanced through his hip. With a curse, he lurched away from the pain, dimly aware of his inability to bear weight on his wounded hip. He glanced back and found the Imperator in a defensive posture, the arkiev in his hand whetted with Admar's blood.

Smoldering burns covered his hairless face. Angry pink blisters lined his lips and eyelids. The mask of stoicism had broken and become wrath.

The jostle of armor and thunder of boots sounded in the distance. *The rest are coming.*

The Imperator's blade swayed like a viper. "I'll flay you myself."

"You said that." Admar rushed him, torch leaving traces of light as he attacked, swinging wildly.

The Imperator aimed a precise blow at Admar's weapon. The tip of his finger sailed away with the torch, but the slave wasn't looking for a duel. He bowled into the Scoth. Chest-to-chest, they flopped back in the dirt and struggled for control of the arkiev. The Imperator's scorched face reeked, an acrid, tangy scent mixed with burnt hair. They battled, spitting and cursing and rousing the dust.

A numb sensation blossomed in Admar's side. Darkness seeped into the edges of his vision. He sucked in a breath and battled his way to position himself atop the smaller man. The hilt of the arkiev pressed up near Admar's shoulder, tangling with his roughspun tunic—he pinned it there with a blood-soaked hand and reared back.

Admar brought his forehead crashing down into the Scoth's face. Bone crunched under his brow. The Imperator snarled through crimson-coated teeth. Admar butted the man again. The Imperator's teeth dug into the bridge of his nose, and the fight seemed to slither from the man. The third time Admar struck, the Scoth's face gave like a spongy mass, and he went limp in the dust.

Disoriented, Admar came to a knee and used the Imperator's own arkiev to cut his throat. He staggered to his feet. Carnage swirled around him.

Danath traded blows nearby with the first of the guards to reach him. A missed swing cost the man. Danath split him from shoulder to navel, one shoulder peeling away from the other. "Namarr!"

The line of slaves pulled. *Crack.* The post gave way. As one, the slaves toppled to the ground. Excited shouts rippled up the line. *They're free.*

Danath raised his ax to the sky. "To the bones!"

The dead were not just for inspiration. They were to provide one last purpose. If they had still been alive, Admar knew they'd have approved.

Slaves flooded into the ditch, chains skittering through the dirt and rustling columns of dust into the murky dawn. Here and there, a Scoth cut his way through the swarm of slaves only to find himself surrounded by a dozen more, all of them armed and hungry for vengeance.

The fear in the guards' eyes was the most beautiful thing Admar had ever seen. The confidence of tyranny fled, beaten back by the will of the righteous.

A hand fell against Admar's shoulder. He twisted around, arkiev cocked back to skewer—

Harcune's face swam before him, all hazy lines. He blinked rapidly, forcing cohesion to form. Her brow was knit together in concern, her voice betraying worry. "You're hurt."

"I'm fine." In truth, strength and feeling leaked from his legs with every heartbeat. Cold lapped at his waist despite the balmy night. Nevertheless, his spirit soared, indomitable. He pushed her gently in the direction of the Scoths. "Go! For freedom!"

Harcune gave a grim nod then flourished a thighbone club. She'd wrapped her chain around her other hand to form a makeshift buckler. Joined by a handful of fellow slaves clambering up out of the ditch, she charged off. "Namarr!" Those who followed echoed her warcry.

Waves of vengeance pounded against the small clusters of Scoth resistance. Slaves gathered into groups of a dozen or more. And then swelled to masses of hundreds. Voar entered the fray, steel rods wreaking havoc for a pointless moment before they were cut down by the endless onslaught of the oppressed.

Admar hobbled behind the rebellion as it flooded into the administrative buildings. When he could go no farther, he eased down onto his knees a stone's throw from the chaos.

The first rays of dawn drifted over Danath's slave army. All that was left of the Scoths were mangled piles of guards and voar. Some had fled while others had barricaded themselves in the barracks.

Torches bobbed through the mob of slaves from the rear to the front. A minute later, flames licked up the side of the building. Frantic shouts followed. The remaining Scoths stumbled forth hacking up smoke and were cut down. They doused the flames just after.

From the same platform the Imperator had addressed Admar's slave crop, Harcune directed the freed men and women to ransack the building for weapons. The larder was to be left untouched. If the rebellion was to continue, they would need supplies, for Danath's dream didn't stop at the liberation of a single camp. It stopped when Scothea was driven from the lands.

This was but the beginning.

Admar had seen as much in Danath's eyes when he had finally convinced him of his plan. Between their slave camp and the others around Unturrus, there numbered nearly ten thousand souls eager for liberation.

Ten thousand souls ready to fight and die.

Admar slumped to one side. Blood-caked, limp hands brushed the earth. Scarlet drenched his knee from the stab wound in his side. He looked up.

Danath took the platform alongside Harcune, broad chest pumping fury. He approached the brass gong, planted a foot against it and shoved it over with a clang. The mob roared approval.

We are not broken...

I am not broken.

Admar's eyes lost focus. The world swooped to his left. Air rushed past—warm, hard ground greeted his right shoulder harshly. His head bounced off the dusty plane. A faint ringing mixed with the distant cheers. Admar wanted to rise with them but couldn't. He blinked, seeing clearly for the last time.

On the platform, tears streamed down Danath's cheeks. He thrust his ax to the heavens. "Namarr!"

Admar smiled. *Unity.*

The war cries of the survivors beat back the ringing in Admar's ears. The songs of the free.

A cool sensation crept up Admar's sides and into his stomach. Moisture leached from his mouth. His throat ached for water but he'd grown accustomed to such a desperate thirst; accustomed in a way none ever should be.

None ever would be again, he hoped.

Hope. It no longer felt dangerous. *Let it go at the grave.* That was the Kanian saying Barnhold always used. Admar understood it now. He didn't need to hold onto hope anymore. It had been loosed, a fast-rising, fast-plunging arrow. Straight into the heart of Scothea.

His hands and legs became weightless and his heart slowed to a peaceful rest. Light faded...

He imagined he was back at the taproom with Lakka and Barnhold. They were laughing, tankards crashing, throwing off the fetters of the downtrodden to capture a few pristine seconds of comfort. Moments of simplicity and honesty among friends. Cherished memories where the pain could not touch.

Admar gasped—a final inhale of dust.

A final taste of freedom.

Afterword

Dear Reader,

I'm honored that you've taken the time to read my novelette. It was a blast to write and I think it serves as a dark, little compliment to the grander works of, "The Price of Power," series.

If you're lamenting the end of "War Song," I have bittersweet news for you. Where one journey ends, another often begins. And so it is here.

The prologue that follows comes from book one of "The Price of Power" series. The original intent was to use it to set the historic stage for a cast of characters different than those you just journeyed with, characters I hope you come to know and love as you continue. But I wanted to note that it was also the inspiration for, "War Song."

While I have no current plans to fill in the nine years that fill the space of Danath's Rebellion, I can easily imagine myself writing those prequel(s) one day.
For now, please enjoy the end of one journey and the beginning of another.

All my best,

MM

EPILOGUE

Namarr, Year 0.

The fear of treachery was rife among them.

Hundreds of nervous rebel lords and ladies bearing steel had cast a shadow over Belara Frost's marriage to Danath Ironlight. Worn as a flat line on every mouth, the threat of betrayal set their eyes to darting and their fingers to twitching over sword hilts. With so many former enemies gathered, Danath's life and his rebellion could be snatched away in an instant.

After the ceremony, all were eager to see the couple hurried off to their tent for consummation.

Duty called them to slide beneath silk covers. Azure eyes met emerald and remained there, unbroken until the fire in their loins cooled, a pact between nations now sealed.

In preparation for the wedding, Belara had been told love was a flower that blossomed with proper care over time, a poetic way of telling her to set her expectations low. She hadn't bothered. Wisdom be damned, she had loved the legend long before she'd met the man. Luckily, her fantasies of their wedding fell far short of the blissful reality. Danath was a man braided of strength and gentleness, honor and passion, caring and command.

Love came easy. The next part would be far more difficult.

Belara coiled around her new husband for a dozen heartbeats before he kissed her forehead and then rolled away to sit at the edge of the bed. His quick departure wasn't upsetting. For the leader and his cause, she'd trained herself to silence the whispers of vanity. She would place her petty desires behind their shared aims, not because her father had commanded it, but because Belara herself yearned for revolution. In order to drive Scothea from the land, Anjuhkar needed to join the war, Belara's precise reason for orchestrating her marriage to Danath in the first place.

The unification of Namarr.

She wanted to spend the hours before dawn running a hand over his broad chest or making love again but couldn't. They were needed in counsel to plan the assault on Alistar.

There was a war to win.

Belara propped herself onto an elbow to watch him dress. Her breath caught at the sight of jagged, glossy scars crisscrossing his back.

Danath's chin hovered over his shoulder. "What is it?"

She pressed a palm against the waxen bolts marring her husband's dark-caramel skin. Smooth. Warm. She imagined what the assault might have looked like, then recoiled. *The injustice done to him and so many like him is unforgivable. How could Scothea think they could keep such a man enslaved?*

He turned, candlelight shimmering across naked muscle. His hand found hers. "You think them horrible?"

She nodded.

A somber smile spread beneath Danath's hawkish nose. "They have shaped me into what I am today. Little did my slave masters know, with every stroke of the whip, every bludgeoning fist, they forged the weapon of their downfall. When I consider it in this way, it isn't all horrible. Any drastic change requires at least some price paid."

Her fists clenched with rage. Mere hours she'd been married and yet the urge to repay the harm done to her husband made her hot with hatred.

Her words came out flat, icy. "They will pay." Blood exacted for dignity stolen.

"Yes...yes." Green eyes regarded her. "But you shouldn't seek retribution for me. Let it be for the others. That was the truer horror. I saw those far weaker than I fall under the slave master's lash, and when they could take no more, voar broke their necks and hurled their broken bodies into the ditches by the nape."

Belara's hands fell to her suddenly queasy stomach. Taking a deep breath, she rushed from the bed, stark naked, unconcerned about the properness of it all. With her shoulders pulled back and her spine rigid, she thrust her chin in the air. She knew then she would do anything and everything her husband asked of her to see the conflict with Scothea brought to an end. Even if it might mean her life. "I apologize, my Prince, for consuming your precious time with idle chit-chat. The convening of the first Namorite Collective commences soon, does it not?"

"It does."

"Then it's best not to make them wait." She started to dress but before she got a leg into her small clothes, Danath was at her side. Taking her hands in his, he brought her around to face him. His grip was firm, comforting, an anchor amid the chaos.

"I am not worthy." She turned away, tears filling her eyes. "I have not shared your struggle."

From slave to rebel prince, Danath Ironlight had claimed his legend. Not once in the previous nine years of war had he faltered. Wherever he went, victory followed. His every bootfall rang with purpose, his every word was a bell's tolling that summoned more warriors to the ranks of the Sons of the Ardent Heart.

He tilted his face down to meet hers. "Do you love me?"

Breath escaped her. She stared at him, knowing her answer but unsure how to make the words perfect enough to convey their depths. "Yes." She choked back tears. "Hearing about you all these years, how could I not? You are everything the world needs and everything I've ever wanted. When I met you, I knew love would be the easiest part."

He knelt, firmly gripping her hand between his. "Then hear this. Today, we may have unified a nation with our marriage, but tomorrow we ensure the freedom of our people. No more bloody backs. No more slaves toiling under foreign masters. We will create a home for the sons and daughters of Namarr...together."

Danath lifted his gaze. "But to you and you alone, I pledge this. With every beat of my heart and every breath the Sempyrean graces me, our love and our lineage will stand as a guardian against evil in the world. Scothea will fall. Namarr will rise."

A tear slid down Belara's cheek. She reached out her hand. "Then let us begin."

A command pavilion towered over the surrounding expanse of soldiers' tents at the end of a wide, mud-caked lane. Belara strode down the thoroughfare with Danath at her side. The various peoples that made up the newly united nation had set aside their old rivalries and now stood shoulder-to-shoulder, saluting the royal couple as they passed.

The sight caused Belara's chest to swell with pride.

Swarthy Lah-Tsarene with skin the color of cinnamon slapped gauntleted fists to the honor plates riding their shoulders, a black hawk or crossed hammers framed in laurels were stitched into their tabards.

Fair-skinned Peladonians of the southern coast bowed at the waist in reverence. These bore the five arrows of the Sempyrean gods on their honor plates.

Belara's own warriors from Anjuhkar cut a fearsome visage in studded leather armor and plated warskirts. Thicker through the joints than the other races of Namarr, the Anjuhks sported dense beards and lustrous manes braided into tight rows of blood-red, flaxen blond, or coal-black hair.

When a Kurg shouldered through to the edge of the lane, Belara failed to hide her shock. The Forgotten People rarely set foot in her homeland, and never had she seen one in person. This man was every bit as stout and broad as she'd heard. Every inch of exposed flesh was golden-hued and te front half of his engorged skull was completely bald, the only hair on his scantily clad body a wild shock of jet erupting from the back of his head.

From the way he said, "Highness," it was clear the common tongue came with great effort.

As word of Danath Ironlight's approach raced ahead of the couple, the number of those lining the path increased. The front row filled in, and then a second, third, and fourth rank of onlookers pressed in tight behind.

A chant started, their breath heaving into the space.

"Namarr!"

Belara and Danath neared the command pavilion where the rest of the rebellion's leaders waited. Flying at five separate points around the command structure, the flag of united Namarr rolled and snapped in the wind, a gauntleted hand crushing a chain in its fist.

Meant to represent my husband's hand.

A hundred menacing warriors stood guard around the pavilion, bathed in torchlight. She glanced back. A cloud of steam formed over the heads of those chanting "Namarr!"

The patriotic masses flooded into the lane in the couple's wake, clapping fists to honor plates in an increasingly rapid rhythm. A crescendo, rising like the tide, thrummed through Belara's bones. Weapons slithered into palms and were thrust toward the night sky. "Namarr!"

Danath caught her eye. Warmth spread through her chest as he was forced to shout to be heard above the din. "Are you ready, my love?"

Belara faced the orange glow emanating from a slit in the canvas. She nodded, and then together, they entered the first meeting of the Namorite Collective.

The ash haft of the Slave Banner stood buried into the earth at the center of the assembly. Braziers sat in each of the five corners of the massive pavilion, their fires bathing those present in a flickering glow. Many were sweating despite the cold. All carried an air of eagerness, a fervor to match Danath's own. With Anjuhkar now pledged to the Sons of the Ardent Heart, victory was within reach.

Swathed head to toe in inky velvet, Malzai D'Alzir took the center of the dusty floor, one hand tucked behind his back. Out of earshot, some called him "Blackwind." Although he'd been the first financier of Danath's revolution, some whispered that his heart lay more in the possible monetary gains of his gambit than a righteous one.

The way Danath had explained it to Belara, the other holders spread rumors about the lord from Kiyahd out of jealousy, for he and Danath were close friends.

The light-brown skin around Malzai's mouth creased as he grinned, exposing stark white teeth. "Please, future lords and ladies of Namarr, let us praise our newly crowned prince, Danath Ironlight, and his illustrious wife, the Ice Maiden, Belara Frost." His voice climbed in register. "Our new Duchess of Anjuhkar!"

The assembly pounded fists to honor plates in a deafening clangor. Danath himself turned to Belara, the fist and broken chain on his shoulder pauldron flashing as he struck it.

"Thank you all," she said once the clamor died. "I want to assure this assembly once more of the dedication Anjuhkar has to you." She glanced at her new husband who looked on impassively. "And to our beloved prince, Danath Ironlight."

A second round of cheers erupted.

"Even now, my father, King Jurna, arrests those Anjuhks who refused to fight against Scothea. This brings me to my first act as Duchess of Anjuhkar, an unpleasant topic but one of utmost necessity." She scanned the semi-circle of bench rows, meeting the eyes of as many hold ladies and lords as she could. "Thirty-five years have passed since the desolation of Kania. My husband's homeland…now little more than a smoking ruin. For thirty-five years, Kanians, Kurgs, and many so-called 'enemies to order' have been murdered or enslaved by Scoths. Some of those you've known. Some of those you've been. For thirty-five years Lah-Tsarra and Peladonia have been subject to Scothea's brutal reign."

Belara's voice rose, reverberating with steel. "I decree that every single one of those Anjuhks opposed to our revolution be imprisoned for thirty-five years. Once their time is served, their bloodlines shall be marked—scarred like we have been—for as many generations as Namarr stands."

Fists pounded honor plates in consensus. A handful stood, mostly bearded Anjuhks, who cast about appealing for affirmation from their peers. Belara thought of the scars on her husband's back and his claim that the greatest suffering had come in watching death descend on those too weak to defend themselves. *My duty is to Danath now. To Namarr. Everything I do must support those aims, even if the consequences weigh heavy.*

She swept forward. The assembly grew quiet as she slowly circled the Slave Banner, studying it. Solicerames, as the Kanians called it, was hewn from the sleeping posts Danath and the other slaves had been chained to each night. A circle of banded wood sat atop a ten-foot pole, and the skins of flayed Scoth slave masters were stretched within. Yellowed with time and smeared with the soot of battle, light bled through the gauntleted fist and broken chain stitched inside the icon.

She dropped to one knee, forehead touching the Slave Banner's haft. "As Duchess of Anjuhkar, I pledge myself, here, now, and always to the Crown of Namarr." Silence and dust swirled behind her as she returned to her place at her husband's side.

A quiet interval passed before Danath spoke. "When we win this war, you know I will not position myself as a tyrant. I stand before you now, a product of the cumulative wisdom and guidance of those gathered here today. Therefore, our new nation will have no king. It will be governed by the voices of its people." He stepped forward. "Through the blood you've willingly shed and the coin you've freely given, I find you all worthy of a seat at the Namorite Collective. However, I have selected the most trusted and capable among you to join myself and my wife, as well as the Monastic Orders, to serve the Collective, Namarr's new governing body!"

Danath cut their cheers short with a wave. Belara knew what came next. She and Danath had discussed it in detail with her father before they'd signed the Unification Treaty. Her eyes found a thin man with a round face and discerning disposition. Sessero Saud.

Danath's tone shifted to be more formal, imperious even. "Sessero, of the House of Saud, will you serve the people of Namarr as Duke of Peladonia?"

The diminutive man saluted Danath, then walked over to Solicerames to repeat the same pledge Belara had.

Once he rejoined the assembly, Danath turned to the man standing at his side. "Malzai D'Alzir, master merchant from the Corridor of Storms. First among my followers. First among my friends. Will you serve the people of Namarr as Duke of Lah-Tsarra?"

Malzai smiled. "It would please me to no end to—"

A Kurg grunted loudly, then parted from the rows of benches. He crossed the intervening space and spat at the feet of the richly dressed Lah-Tsarene merchant. A litany of jeers rained.

With steely calm, Danath stepped between Malzai and the bristling Kurg. Belara noted that, like the rest of his kind, he was shorter than most Namorites, broader than all, and with amber skin that was strange to behold.

"Easy, Tondarro." Danath placed a hand firmly against the Kurg's thick chest. "What troubles you?"

The Kurg's chiseled face swung toward Danath. "I mean no offense to you, my Prince." The common tongue flowed naturally from his lips. "But to *him*, I give all of it."

"Malzai D'Alzir is now a Duke of Namarr," said Danath. "He represents me and the Crown to which you swore yourself. Your actions *do* offend me. On the eve of my wedding, the eve of our victory, you spur chaos. We may have shed Scoth blood together, but I warn you, I'll brook no disruptions to our mission."

"My Prince, this man's reputation..." Tondarro looked to the dusty floor, massive chest heaving with rage, then snorted. "Long before he was your friend, the blood of a thousand Kurgs colored his hands. Could you choose no other?"

Danath gave a somber smile. "The past dies today, Tondarro. When we were a fractured nation, all of us here were foes. Those days are no longer. Tomorrow will be different. As will every tomorrow thereafter. Scothea faces its last sunset as rulers of our land." The leader of the Sons of the Ardent Heart raised his voice for all to hear. "Besides, you too will take a seat on the Namorite Collective."

The Kurg's head jerked up, his brow furrowed in disbelief.

Murmurs broke out among those gathered. Danath ignored them. "Lord Malzai himself suggested it."

Inwardly, Belara smiled. The move to seat a Kurg on the Namorite Collective was brilliant; it ensured peace beyond the numbered days of the revolution. Kurgs fought alongside the Sons of the Ardent Heart out of necessity, making their allegiance tentative at best and likely to last only so long as Scothean occupation did.

Danath clapped a hand on the chieftain's bare, blocky shoulder. "Tondarro of the Moon Clan, will you represent the Kurgish enclaves?"

Tondarro glowered at Malzai. Corded neck muscles twitched as he shook his head. "The River and Forest enclaves cannot have agreed to this."

A rush of sound and air pulled Belara's attention to the back of the pavilion where a dark figure materialized from a black cloud. He spoke with a deep, gravelly voice to match his imposing visage. "They will."

All eyes turned to the man wreathed in otherworldly shadow as darkness dilated into a blot behind him and then dissipated. Blood pounded in Belara's ears. She touched her throat a split second before a score of others gasped with her in unison. A word circulated the assembly—spoken low as if sacred.

Awakened.

The hulking man strode past the rows of seated rebel lords, black vapor leaking from his eyes. The rich and the dangerous alike made way. Benches dragged hastily backward, kicking up dust. He came to a stop, turned, blinking at the fear in his wake. The inky vapor dissipated, revealing flint-hard eyes.

The man was a Kurg, same as Tondarro, but that was where the similarities stopped.

From the nose up, the Awakened's face was tattooed black but for a circle of untouched golden flesh around one eye. The massive horns of an ebhor curled down and thrust outward around a ram's head helm. Most Kurgs wore little. This one dressed like a priest. Robes of dark maroon swathed him and slithered across the ground, a whisper heralding his coming.

Understanding clicked into place as Belara noticed a thousand symbols of eyes, flames, and hands stitched in gold and covering his robes.

Pockets of debate swept the assembly as others recognized the significance. Not just any Awakened. A Dominarri. For as long as Belara could remember, she'd heard stories about the mysterious religious order of supernatural beings that had been in hiding since Scothea's invasion thirty-five years earlier. Never had she met one.

"Darkhorn." Tondarro's mouth fell open, his voice husky with awe. "It can't be."

Impassive as a pillar, the Awakened dismissed the chieftain's gawking with a definitive wave. "I have advised the leaders of the Forest and River enclaves to accept you as the Kurgish representative. None will deny it." He inclined his head at Tondarro. "Nor will you."

The chieftain licked his lips then bowed before making his way to the Slave Banner. He knelt, kissed it, spoke the pledge, then cast a last look of reverence in Darkhorn's direction before returning to his seat. Belara wondered how much of the man's veneration was driven by fear.

"Darkhorn is here at my behest. A powerful ally." Danath pumped a fist at his side. "Friends, take heart! The Dominarri have returned from hiding. Tomorrow they send twenty of their best to aid us. Scothea *will* fall."

A single detractor cried out amid the din of triumphant shouting. Danath frowned and searched the crowd. "Oka Bael? Are you truly opposing the help of the Dominarri?" Danath glanced at Belara. The Bloodbull, Oka Bael, was one of her people—the most famous Anjuhk to dedicate himself to Danath Ironlight's rebellion.

The charcoal-bearded Anjuhk stood, shrugging ox-like shoulders. With a forlorn expression, he stared down at the head of a vicious-looking two-handed maul in his grasp. The way he handled the weapon made it seem a toy. The man sniffled as if about to cry. He was met with little sympathy and many glares.

Oka Bael picked at the head of his maul like a weary toddler. "I'm sad, my Prince. So very sad..." He stifled a chuckle, his momentary facade of sorrow shattered. "What will I do when all the Scoths are dead?"

Those around the Bloodbull rolled their eyes and laughed. The Anjuhk threw up a hand. "I'm sincere! My friends, I grieve! A future without Scoths to kill is no future at all." A lord named Lydo Olabran seated beside Oka dragged him back to sitting by the hem of his mail shirt.

The room broke into raucous laughter.

Danath remained stoic. When Belara saw this, she fell silent. A hundred lords and ladies followed suit.

"Oka, my friend. While I share your vehemence for justice, I cannot be so mirthful yet." Danath surveyed the room. "There is still work to be done. Much work."

He stepped into the semi-circle of benches and came to a stop before Oka Bael, then indicated for him to rise. "Do you see this man, this courageous man? I would see his hammer killing cows. Not voar. Not raeks. Not Scoths. I would see all of your futures bright. Your nights peaceful. I will sleep easy once I know your blades and hammers fall to rust above your hearths. Then my friend," he turned, gripping the monstrous Anjuhk's shoulders, "then and only then will I laugh with you. I will dance at your side rather than fight at it."

Danath retook the center of the room. Heart thundering, Belara held her breath. Sweat slicked the area between her shoulders. Leather armor creaked and chain jostled as those highborn dressed for war shifted in their seats, the passion and magnitude of their leader drawing them forth.

"We have the power of the Dominarri at our backs. Darkhorn himself!" Danath shouted. "We have the strength of purpose in our arms! The spirit of our fallen brothers and sisters in our hearts! Heroes, one and all! The gods of the Sempyrean themselves could not stop us now." Hoarse cries broke across the assembly. A score or more stood and clapped. "Tomorrow, when we attack Alistar, remember this…"

In a single movement, Danath Ironlight wrested Solicerames from the earth and heaved the standard heavenward, its wooden icon nearly brushing the pavilion's pinnacle.

"Shackles only hold those who allow it! One who does not seek to break their chain is already broken by it! Here and now, free your swords! Free your souls! My sons and daughters of Namarr, you cannot die but once. Let us live boldly and without fear!"

In answer, cheers cascaded all around. Belara's heart was in her throat, and then it hurtled forward as she threw the weight of her hopes into the space. Oka Bael rushed from the benches, ripped off his mail then tore open his shirt, howling at the ceiling. Lydo Olabran raised a hammer in each fist and clanged them together, a sharp ringing barely heard. Malzai D'Alzir grinned broadly, teeth glimmering in the braziers' light while Darkhorn watched the uproar with grim neutrality.

"The Dawn Tower falls tomorrow!" Danath's voice boomed above the fury, words like thunderclaps. "And from the ashes, Namarr rises! Rises! Rises!"

Swords sang from sheaths. A fast tattoo of fists slammed against honor plates, drowning out all other sound. Tears streamed down Belara Frost's cheeks.

Death could not touch them, those fire-hearted gods. They were invincible. Fathers and mothers to a birth unrivaled in its momentous conception.

The birth of Namarr.

ABOUT AUTHOR

Michael Michel lives in Bend Oregon with the love of his life and their two children. When he isn't obsessively writing, editing, or doing publishing work, he can be found exercising, coaching leaders in the corporate world, and dancing his butt off at amazing festivals like Burning Man. His favorite shows are Dark, The Wire, and Barry. He loves nature and deep conversations with—anyone really—and few things bring him more joy than a couple of hours playing table tennis.

BUY BOOK ONE & CONTINUE THE JOURNEY:

https://www.amazon.com/Price-Power-Book-1/dp/B0BTKZPNF9

REVIEWS:

If you enjoyed this novelette and feel it should find its way into the hands of as many readers as possible, please leave a review on Goodreads, Amazon, or wherever else you feel called to share. And talk to other fantasy readers in your community about it! No matter what, I deeply appreciate your support.

SOCIAL MEDIA:

Instagram - @michaelmichelauthor

Website – https://michaelmichelauthor.com/

Twitter - @Michael__Michel (two dashes in the center there)

www.ingramcontent.com/pod-product-compliance
Lightning Source LLC
Chambersburg PA
CBHW020051310726

48970CB00007B/2510